Around Distant Suns

Around Distant Suns

Nine Stories Inspired by Research from the
St Andrews Centre for Exoplanet Science

Edited by Emma Johanna Puranen

GUARDBRIDGE BOOKS
ST ANDREWS, SCOTLAND

Published by Guardbridge Books,
St Andrews, Fife, United Kingdom.

http://guardbridgebooks.co.uk

AROUND DISTANT SUNS

"The Stripped Core" © 2021, Colin Bramwell
"Glossary" © 2021, Emma Bussi
"Soonest Mended" © 2021, Honor Hamlet
"One Cloud at a Time" © 2021, Priyanka Jha
"Rise In Perfect Light" © 2021, Maeghan Klinker
"A Momentary Brightening" © 2021, Laura Muetzelfeldt
"After Colour" © 2021, Kiale Palpant
"A Spark In a Flask" © 2021, Emma Johanna Puranen
"Cloudgazing" © 2021, Guy Woods

Cover Image: © 2021, Tinne De Vis

ISBN: 978-1-911486-65-7

Table of Contents

Introduction

Emma Johanna Puranen

I always thought being a science consultant for a major motion picture sounded like the coolest job in the world. Imagine—working with a writer or a director to figure out how that time machine might work, or what that black hole might look like, or which colours of light those aliens would see. When I found out that the reality of being a science consultant is usually sitting down for a single conversation with a filmmaker, answering some questions, never hearing from them again and learning the results along with everyone else when the movie comes out—I was a little disappointed, to say the least.

What might happen if science consultants were more involved in the creative process? Last December, I decided I wanted to find out. I have no sway over Hollywood, but I *am* able to get together a group of creative writers and a group of exoplanet scientists. I asked around at the St Andrews Centre for Exoplanet Science, where I am a doctoral student, and soon enough I had experts in astrobiology, gravitational microlensing, Miller-Urey experiments, and exoplanet atmospheres on board. A few e-mail exchanges with the School of English introduced me to a talented crew of writers. Everyone was up to the challenge and adventure, eager to share their art and their science.

I paired writers and researchers, and over the course of a few months each pair met several times. They got to know each other and then discussed the researcher's work, tossing around story ideas and looking for a spark. I emphasised that the researcher had to remain involved throughout the process, not just at the beginning, though I left the details of how that might work up to each pair. Other than the story needing to be inspired by the research, I gave very little guidance as to what to write—I wanted to see what each pair would come up with. And my trust could not have been better-placed—the results of these creative exchanges are the nine incredible stories, poems, and radio plays in the volume before you.

Now, I believe science fiction authors are under no obligation to "get the science right"—their works are fiction for a reason—and yet, I have heard many of them express that they *want* to. Real science, after all, often inspires their works, and many science fiction authors are the types who read popular science articles and eagerly follow NASA missions. As well, science fiction is extremely influential, and can be used as a tool for public outreach and science communication—one that avoids the immediate eyes-glazing-over response that accompanies the rolling out of an equation-covered blackboard. For example, take a quick poll of your friends: how many have heard of Kepler-16b? How many have heard of Tatooine? Both are circumbinary exoplanets—an exoplanet is a planet outside our solar system, and a circumbinary one orbits around two stars—but the fictional planet is much better-known than the real planet. Even if people aren't acquainted with the jargon-heavy term "circumbinary exoplanet", they already understand the concept perfectly—thanks to science fiction. Scientists took advantage of this familiar teaching tool in press releases when Kepler-16b's discovery was announced, calling it a "Tatooine planet".

Scientists do a lot of *computer modelling*—that is, setting certain parameters, like, say, the temperature and chemical makeup of an atmosphere—and then running simulations to see what will happen. In my example, that would be how the atmosphere might change over time. Science fiction writers are *also* running models—but instead of "if the temperature is set to X, what will the wind speeds be?" or "is molecular oxygen stable in the long term in this atmosphere?" their models focus on human reactions, addressing questions like "how would society change if scientists successfully create life in a lab?" or "what would it feel like to be educated in cryosleep?" Ultimately, both groups are addressing deeper questions—*what is life, where did we come from, are we alone, what does it all mean* — from different angles.

I encouraged the pairs to think about where to stay realistic, where to be plausible, and where to make things up. All three of these are important, and science should serve as an inspiration and a guide, but it is not a limiter for fiction. On the contrary, the mantra "truth is stranger than fiction" is often applicable—why set all your stories on copy-pasted Earths when you can visit a hot Jupiter? These gas giants orbit blisteringly close to their host stars, and until they were first discovered in the 1990s, they were thought to go against the rules of solar system formation. Science opens up a plethora of new ideas for stories, settings, plots, and characters.

We are living in an era of unprecedented discovery of exoplanets. The first ones were discovered just over two decades ago, and since then, we have found thousands. This is an incredibly exciting time to be an exoplanet researcher, and we at the Centre for Exoplanet Science have been busier than ever (to learn more about our work, visit us at https://exoplanets.wp.st-andrews.ac.uk/). The stories in this volume capture the joys, the frustrations, and the sheer wonders that accompany straining your eyes to search for other worlds, and for hints at life. Humanity has just barely opened our eyes to the universe, and our vision is still adjusting to the dark. Exoplanet science is a field that is no stranger to the unknown, so we understand the rewards—and the *necessity* — of interdisciplinarity, of making our own science richer for collaborating with experts from other subjects. Science fiction is a crucial tool for learning about how humans might interact with these far-off planets—after all, science fiction writers have been writing en masse about exoplanets a good deal longer than scientists.

The Impalpable

Our cover art is the brilliant work 'The Impalpable' by Belgian artist Tinne De Vis. Her piece is part of the Ex(p)oplanet project at the Interdisciplinary Studio at SLAC Leuven. Ex(p)oplanet is itself a bridge between art and science, bringing together astrophysicists from the CHAMELEON project, who are researching the origins and atmospheres of exoplanets, with art students to broaden horizons and address the question 'How can art and science meet, strengthen and challenge each other, and propose new insights?'

In Tinne's own words, the cover illustration is 'a future box displaying wild exoplanetary elements', in this case based on the real exoplanet Tau Ceti f, representing 'a lightyears' sensation at this tiny restricted moment'.

The Stripped Core

Writer: Colin Bramwell
Researcher: Dominic Samra

Now that I am approaching the final stages of life, I find myself thinking more and more about the kind of world we have made for our children. How often do men of my age tell us that they regret nothing? An irresponsible cliché, to my mind. A fallback position for those incapable of examining their own lives critically, even. If I could live my time on this planet again, avoiding the innumerable mistakes that I have made in the course of my existence, I would see it as my responsibility do so.

In the last war, I lost an eye and gained a son. I have tried to instil a sense of purpose in the boy. Although Alex performs reasonably well at school, he gives the impression of being lazy and incurious. Many of his report cards describe him as 'a dreamer'. It's not that he doesn't do well! It's that he often forgets to look up, if you catch my meaning. The benefits of Exterior Schooling to such a boy are unquestionable. I am particularly impressed with the 'stripped core' initiation, which feels to me like a purposive advancement of 'gaming development' for children of his age. In your prospectus, I found the following: 'a sense of responsibility, of stakes being raised, is greatly missed from this new post-war generation of ours.' A sentiment not so often expressed so directly these days, but I am in complete agreement. Despite his shortcomings, my son is a capable young man in top physical condition, and should have no problems with the cryoeducative aspects of transport to The Exterior. In this, and in many other ways, I believe that Alex is an ideal candidate for your scholarship programme. Please do find all relevant paperwork affixed.

* * *

'Like the deepest recesses of the Marianas Trench, the great core of the gas giant is shrouded in a mysterious darkness: a darkness that exists in a state of constant motion. In order to reach this core—a "journey to the centre of Jupiter"—we would need a submersible craft.'

The episode was almost over. As retro-synth music for the closing credits swelled into the monologue, the water in Alex's tank turned purple. The show's narrator—a famous, long-dead American scientist—continued:

'As with early explorations into the depths of that trench, this craft would need to be remotely operated, capable of withstanding great temperatures and unimaginably strong winds. Our submersible would move through layers of hydrogen in various physical states: gas, liquid, metallic. Its pilot would have to navigate a thick soup of electrons in order to reach the core. And then, once this journey through seas of cloud and hydrogen was completed, and we finally reached our Ithaca—the centre of the great giant—where would we find ourselves? On yet another surface. For the rock would surely have a centre, too: another layer, another core...'

* * *

Alex had figured out that there must be two other students in his dorm. In the brief periods of consciousness between lessons, he watched the ceiling. Over a number of years, light from the tanks danced in colours above him. As time went on, he began to make out the silhouettes of the other students on the ceiling, behind the tank-lit water.

The cryoeducation tanks—the Academy's prospectus referred to these as 'floating classrooms'—were designed to blur the lines between normal conscious and unconscious learning processes. Students would emerge from the tanks with a reasonably complete grounding in all human knowledge. Though the emphasis of their learning was largely placed on engineering, all other conceivable subjects were covered in the syllabus. Literature, history and music were particular strengths of the Chthonian Academy, and stressed as important subjects for students to master, in preparation for their final exam. Not that mastery was a choice. After so many years of passive learning, even at lightspeed, it would be impossible for students to forget the knowledge they had acquired. It was burned into their brains through repetition.

Alex felt the cold of the sedative move up from his feet, through his body, like a wave. In a few minutes he would be out cold, starfishing once again in the tank, returned to a state of unconscious rest for however many days before the next lesson. He checked the status of their journey on the map. Seven hundred lightyears to TOI-849b: a little under halfway. Alex wrapped his hand around the breathing tube like a baby, and fell into sleep, or something close to it.

* * *

Alex couldn't tell if it was a film or a dream, and he wasn't entirely sure that he cared much either way. Whatever the thing was, it told the story of a boy from London who moves to Northumberland at the age of seven. On the drive up, his family car exits the motorway, and the boy sees the stars for the first time. He asks Santa Claus for a telescope. Wiki pages and JPEGs of diagrams loading slowly on dial-up internet. The inspiring physics teacher explaining gravity to a class of students, only one of whom is paying close attention. The Kepler telescope launch. Revision, exams, university, lectures, libraries, labs, exams, funding applications. The boy studies for a doctorate in physics: he swaps his telescope for an observatory with large amounts of light pollution, but finds out quickly that his own research will not require him to look at the stars. Kepler has detected thousands of new, distant planets, and exoplanetology has exploded as a discipline. After Kepler, the idea of an individual astronomer with a telescope becomes romantic: these things are more often done in teams. In a fit of contrarian bravery, however, the boy begins to sneak into the observatory, night after night, in order to try and figure something out about the Interior. He focuses on the nearest gas giant, Jupiter. He begins to obsess over the core of the planet. Trips back and forth to the observatory. Analyses of clouds over Jupiter. Blackboards full of equations. Long days reading article after article. Images of stripped cores from Kepler. The boy's hand, turning the dials on the sixties-style interface of the observatory. Arguments with colleagues and a disbelieving supervisor. A long-suffering wife who tells the boy that she believes in him and that he should never give up. The breakthrough. The Prize, the acceptance speech. 'All we care about is telling people what we know. There's scope for telling people instead why they should care. The job of scientists is not just to know: it's to inspire. What enables us to move forward as a species is not the things we acquire: it's the ability to imagine a world beyond mere acquisition. Humanity has spent too long looking *down*: at books, equations, our feet, the ground. It's time to look *up*.'

* * *

Striplights flickered on overhead and the lids to the tanks slowly opened. The bioluminescent water thickened and turned a shade of light pink. Alex pulled his shoulders free from the slime, and sat with his back exposed to the chilly air of his dorm. He breathed heavily, staring at his feet, for about ten minutes. Then he looked up, and saw the dorm-room in full detail. One curtain made a semicircle around his tank. It was emblazoned with the Chthonic Academy crest: a rock with an angel's wings, backgrounded by stars. Ahead, there was a small changing area, with a mannequin wearing full school uniform. And further, the door to the room, above which text on a large screen was flashing green. THE FINAL EXAM WILL COMMENCE IN EXACTLY ONE HOUR.

From behind the curtain to his left, a loud, wet slap, and a groan. With some difficulty, Alex swung his legs out of the thickening gloop, and lifted his skinny frame out of the tank, and onto a small platform beside it. As soon as he had shifted his weight fully onto this platform, hot water fell onto his body, dissolving the tank slime. He could still hear the sound of struggling. Trying his best to ignore this for now, he rose to his feet, walked over to the mannequin, dried and dressed himself. He struggled gainfully with his tie for a few minutes. Only after executing the perfect double windsor did he allow himself to walk around to the curtain to his left, where another boy, completely naked and covered in tank-syrup, was trying and failing to get to his feet. The boy was somehow even skinnier than Alex: almost emaciated, with long, light-brown hair. He had crawled out of the bath on the wrong side, and fallen onto the metal floor. His legs had taken the fall and were purple all over. Alex offered him a hand up, and helped him round to the platform where he could shower. Then he looked around the curtain to his right. The tank was shut, the water inside remained luminescent. Another student looked to be sleeping within.

A loud beep. Alex looked around at the screen above the door. REPORT TO THE EXAM HALL.

'Are you ready?'

Alex pivoted round to see the skinny, long-haired boy limping towards him. He looked uncomfortable in his uniform, which was clearly intended for a much larger boy.

'This one hasn't opened.'

'Not our problem. We have to get going.'

'I'll mention it to the invigilator.'

'What's your name?'

'Alex. Yours?'

'Cairn. Listen, Alex, thanks for the help back there, but—'

'I won't make a habit of it.'

'I'd appreciate that.'

The door opened into a corridor, windowless and impossibly bright. Alex and Cairn were quickly absorbed into a sea of students that flowed down towards the examination hall.

* * *

The room was set out like a gigantic amphitheatre: a red velvet curtain was drawn across its stage, and the seats looked as though they were made of old stone. The students spread out along its length, up and down its corridors, until all were seated. Alex and Cairn sat together. They'd barely said a word to each other on their walk down the corridor. On each seat was a small bag containing earphones and gloves. Written on the bag was the instruction: DO NOT OPEN UNTIL EXAM COMMENCES. Looking around, Alex couldn't help but notice that a few of the seats were empty. He started counting them. Once he had reached thirty, the curtains opened, revealing what first looked to Alex like a painting. It took him a few seconds to realise that he was in fact looking out of a gigantic window, at a planet.

Alex instantly recognised this planet as the stripped core of a gas giant. The layers of atmosphere that he had heard described in cryoeducative documentaries had been almost blown away entirely by the nearest star. He could see the skeletal outline of a tail, facing away from the brilliantine sun: the last stage of hydrodynamic escape, almost complete. It was like watching someone take a long, final breath. Alex was enraptured: the impending realities of the exam, which he had been extensively prepared for in his tank, were almost forgotten. He stared at the planet, tried to imagine it in its former glory. The immensity of the gas giants he had encountered on television screens, shrunk to a pip. He recalled from the tank an image of the clouds on the planet's surface: the existence of planet-sized clouds on the night side of the planet, how they danced over the darkening reds, the garnets and blush colours of hydrogen, flaring on the illuminated side under inconceivable heat. Bands of cloud being pulled from night to daylight so strong it snuffed them out entirely. The words from the documentary came back to Alex. *Another layer, another core.* He went to touch the stone of his amphitheatre seat, but his hand met the bag containing the exam equipment, reminding him of where he was, of what he was about to undertake. He shut his eyes and took a deep breath. There was the vague sense of feeling watched: not by anyone else in the room, but by the planet itself. Alex was reminded of his father's glass eye. He had stood in the panelled study and pleaded with his father not to send him away. He had looked into his father's eyes, and for a second he thought he had broken through. Then he saw his father's working eye roll slowly upwards to the ceiling, and knew there was nothing more to be said, to be done. What had disturbed him then, moreso even than the man's seemingly total indifference to his son's desperation, was that the eye of glass remained fixed on him, in an impression of sympathy, even after his father's eye had looked away. Now, the stripped core stared back at him with the same familiar indifference.

The school song came blaring over the speakers, and the students rose to their feet. *Build, build, up!* they sang. The examination was about to begin. Over nine hours, the students of the 78th Chthonian Academy would build their school across the night side of the stripped core. Acres of barren rock would be terraformed into pristine arable land, to be tilled under a heat and light-resistant dome. The results of the exam would thus be provided to the students instantaneously: if any student failed, all of their work would be evaporated instantly by the heat. Alex had undergone thousands of years of cryoeducation, and still he felt unprepared. Nervously, he opened the bag, and put on the gloves first, then the earphones. A voice was whispering, in both ears. 'Look up. Look up. Look up.' Alex tilted his head back. He remembered the other student in his dorm, still asleep in the tank. He had thought to inform an invigilator. Too late. The same voice—a deep, woman's voice—was counting down from ten. A battalion of tiny ships would be launched from the hull, towards the stripped core that would become their home. He could feel the twin controllers in his gloved hands now: he gripped them, and beams of light moved from both headphones, meeting in the centre of his face, masking his features in light. He was in the cockpit. He abandoned himself to the moment, to his instincts, as taught. His tiny ship was fired out of the hull, along with the rest. The exam hall filled with the screams of students. Alex screamed too. All of space loomed ahead. The eye of the stripped core grew bigger and bigger. Alex forgot about his father, about the other student in the tank. He surrendered to the task at hand. He gave himself a second to meet the blind planet's gaze head-on, and then set to work.

COLIN BRAMWELL is a writer and performer from the Black Isle, in the north of Scotland. His poetry has been published in *Bella Caledonia*, *Gutter*, *The Scotsman* and *Northwords Now*. His first pamphlet of poems, *The Highland Citizenship Test*, was published by Stewed Rhubarb in May of 2021; his latest show, *Umbrella Man*, toured in the UK, Australia, and New Zealand. He is currently studying for a PhD in Scots, poetry and translation at the University of St Andrews.

From Colin: I greatly enjoyed the process of collaborating with Dominic on this story. Our collaboration was shaped by two meetings; in the first, Dominic told me about his research, and we spoke about how he came to study exoplanets. He also gave me some fascinating descriptions of how a stripped core might look, as well as a primer on gas giants. Dominic communicated a number of complicated points about science to me in a way that felt very understandable; during the course of our meeting, we spoke about the need for effective science communication to the public at large, and so this point became a guiding principle for me in writing the story: I didn't want to go too far into the scientific aspects, instead looking to the contents of our meeting for inspiration. We communicated over email, and had another meeting in late March to finalise a few changes – Dominic was also very helpful at the editorial stages, making a number of observations that turned out to be very useful for the story. We were both reasonably happy with how it turned out: a very pleasant and fun collaboration, all in all.

DOMINIC SAMRA, originally from Lincolnshire in England, is a PhD student in the Centre for Exoplanet Science at the University of St Andrews. The dark skies inspired a keen interest in astronomy from a young age, and whilst studying physics at Imperial College London, Dominic always intended to go into exoplanet research. Dominic's current research focuses on the specific physical processes governing the way that cloud particles form in gas-giant exoplanets. As well as this, he studies the distribution of clouds on a class of planets called ultra-hot Jupiters, which, like the name suggests, are similar in size and mass to Jupiter but can be incredibly hot because they orbit much closer to their stars. The clouds that form on these planets are unlike anything we see on Earth, made up of the same minerals that form quartz, rubies, sapphires and diamonds.

From Dominic: I was excited to work with Colin on this as I wanted to see what the use of fiction could do to not only explain the science, but also to inspire people to take interest in what can be a niche field. In particular I thought there was real potential for outreach, to capture the attention of people who are normally turned off by dry descriptions of the scientific details. I am really glad that Colin picked up this concept and ran with it, whilst also incorporating a wide range of atmosphere science. I think he did a wonderful job of distilling our quite in-depth conversations into a plethora of 'jumping off points' for the audience, should they have their interest piqued by one of his vivid descriptions. Overall the experience of this collaboration has been eye-opening in moving away from descriptivism and really pulling out the beauty of the science.

GLOSSARY

Writer: Emma Bussi
Researcher: Professor Christiane Helling

I am trying to write about the clouds
And the downpour of light
They can allow

Someone made a glossary for this years ago
A collected explanation of words
That I can't seem to find

A glossary is
The more time
The more people and light

The downpour meant that we could also see up
Through

The object of study in the glossary
Exists outside of the object we are in

The object we are looking at
Curves past our light-blue atmosphere
And screaming stars

An image of this is rarely
(If ever)
Reliable
But I've met a few people who try and make it as beautiful

As when you let your tongue
Graze the top of your mouth
Unsure about what to say next

There is also uncertainty in the glossary
Though a cloud may be too boastful to ever let
The experience of such an emotion be apparent

That something else you sometimes feel
Is nothing other than the debris a cloud
Has left you with

The glossary was revised years ago

By people who held a different perception of light
All I know is that it was no longer a downpour
But a concentrated point

And it blinked so we knew it was real
Maybe it was just trying to prove it was alive

This is where I become too sentimental
I will try and avoid rhyme

I vaguely remember the glossary encouraging
Those who want to write about clouds
To practice the act of unveiling in their everyday

So we may get better at unveiling a cloud

To unveil is to change the course of covering
It is a widely-held belief that this act
Only happens with eyes present

But if you listen to the words we use
To describe any action
You will unveil what we are really trying to say

I trusted the glossary and documented all my attempts:

Thursday, April 1, 2021 3:42:23 PM GMT+01:00
Unveil a dull headache
into an evening

Tuesday, May 13, 2008 2:42:23 PM GMT+01:00
Unveiling my desires to bathe in my dreams

I have also tried flirting with a cloud
In the hopes of inversing this unfair power dynamic

Clouds don't care if you're watching

I have reacted badly to the rejection
And accused it of being too frail a mind
To ever receive my light-hearted probing

If you want to understand the object we are looking at
You have to pick at the gap
Like what Barthes said
Is not the body's most erotic zone there where the garment leaves gaps?

I always imagine a lone leg revealed in the slit of a dress
Leaving gaps behind itself as we trail it
Gaps in teeth and conversations
The gaps of particles

I am picking at the gaps between particles

The cloud is caught in perpetual metamorphosis
Always another variation of itself
An impasse it can never get out of

The glossary has words like unveil
Because it is trying to find a gap in clouds
So that we can appreciate those further planets
The object of our study

If you want to grasp any relationship
Refer to its glossary
You will see the history of a person's attempt
To try and understand everything

EMMA BUSSI is a poet and MLitt student at St Andrews. Their research interests include trans poetics and the diaries of Paul Klee.

PROFESSOR CHRISTIANE HELLING is a Professor in Physics & Astronomy at the University of St Andrews, and she is the director of the St Andrews Centre for Exoplanet Science. Christiane's research involves the study of exoplanet atmospheres with very different weather and climate than Earth, places where clouds made of mineral particles and exolightning form. Her research on exoplanets is very interdisciplinary, and leads her to conclude that only if we communicate across disciplinary boundaries will we be able to understand what exoplanets truly mean for humanity. Christiane will become the director of the Institute of Space Research of the Austrian Academy of Science in October 2021.

From Christiane: Collaborating with an artist to convey a deeper understanding of my research through poetry was mind-opening and a humbling experience alike. I am intrigued by the depth of understanding of a subject that is required in order to be able to capture the subject within the limited number of the words of a poem. It turns out that writing a poem is very similar to writing a scientific paper: precise wording and a clear structure are the key for conveying the message. Our collaboration was driven by the wish to let others participate in the fascination for our own craft.

SOONEST MENDED

Writer: Honor Hamlet
Researcher: Till Kaeufer

The universe is filled by what it is most likely to be filled by
The simplest things are the most likely things to fill themselves
The shortest things are happiest. I write plot like dot on the graph.

Dancing fighting making are all things that can be done pretty well unskilled.
The green rushes on the bank are like this, not altogether. A floor, a floor then
low and scraped and packed down with muted barks and undead leaves
A robin flies across the furthest corner.

What is most regular is random, it clumps. Heat is the heart eating
Distance is like personality means influence, running fine creases round the eyes
No I mean, influence is a kind of interpretation,
Understanding through ratios. Like two blocks about the same height
One of me and other of the raisin
In this way we can be far apart, in fact the farther away
The more acutely rationalised. Before it is only one thing and none other,
and so not at all understood.

Brushing teeth like sewing seeds crooked in the furrow
It is, you say, this is. Habitational force of soft impressions
The impressionistic state of habit
Flour everywhere, a block in my breath and tiny piles on the counter
Huge against gas, yet held within a breadth
We are unused to with our bready limitations, and markers on the screen.

A scene itself shows
The puffiness of disappointment, in an ill-concealed collapse
But the same inversion contains something so
bulbous and buttery as the opposition between magnets

and the cloud is tugged down to a disc
by roundening that
curves like how *would* I know what I want

Then the floor, tidied of leaves round the edges
its cleanness tempting concavities or convexities
yet still ungainly, as we make a line of best fit
through the uneven diamond dots. You look in the mirror
at the lightness of the things around you and the bovine
reality of your features. They say whatever it is it should be a good job
the data looking like
the puffiness of your cheeks,
the yellow tone in my eyeballs, red traces of capillaries.

The sun itself is something like
Green upon green, the opposition of similarity constantly contested
and improbably, so improbably overcome it is not in fact 'possible'
Yet of course, unskilled
taking a shortcut, being the thickness of something completely different,
doubling your colour in that instant.
What I mean is
To be so small as to be 'appearance' entirely, all the way through
Single strand of hair in a rainbow mane
/everything personal
Like my fire fingers will not burn
in playing abstract board games

HONOR HAMLET is studying for an Mlitt in Poetry at St Andrews, having completed a bachelor's in Fine Art at Te Whare Wananga o Tamaki Makaurau, New Zealand. Her research is miscellaneous, including interests in religious phenomena and found texts.

From Honor: I found the process really fun, Till was very generous with his time. I do sometimes work with scientific information, so I have been curious to learn more for a while. As is apparent in the poem I was particularly fascinated by how such vast areas are taken up with such tiny molecules; hydrogen and helium being the easiest to make. That such things begin incompletely and are formed/stabilised through fixing themselves is an appealing idea to me. As a parallel to this concept, I leant on American poet John Ashbery's poem *Soonest Mended*, a debt of course shown in my own title. The role of dust in beginning a solar system also opened up intriguing questions of scale for me. Till's work with machine learning helped in writing the tail end of this poem. I found a program that machine learns written text and Till installed and ran it. I very much wanted to include the phrase 'upslope dinosaur' that was generated, but in the end it was too potent. In the final stanza I take the example of quantum-tunnelling in the sun to consider how things that are very difficult can also be completely easy given the chance, linking up with the ease of hydrogen that first interested me—though on the opposite end of the scale of likelihood. Stylistically I wanted something that reflected the deductive/schematic approach of science, and also presented some challenges to it. I hoped that it would be something Till or other researchers might enjoy, so I also factored that into the process.

TILL KAEUFER is a PhD student in Astrophysics at the University of St Andrews. His research focuses on the disks around young stars in which planets form. While modern modelling software is good at predicting how these disks look like based on shape parameters, running one model takes a lot of time. This makes it impossible to run many models while constantly comparing them to real observations to find the best model, and also calculate the confidence in this model. Till tries to solve this problem by training different machine learning techniques like neural networks to predict the look of disks based on the same input that is given to modelling programs.

From Till: During the writing process, we found many similarities between writing a poem and training a neural network. While writing a poem, you're constantly asking if the information in the previous line is relevant enough to trigger a reaction in the next line. This is exactly how neural networks work. This makes the poem format so fitting that Honor included one line in the poem that was written by a neural net.

One Cloud at a Time

A Radio Play

Writer: Priyanka Jha
Researcher: Nanna Bach-Møller

NB: *Italics* indicate stage directions.

CHARACTERS:

Dr Bach: Woman in her late twenties (at the start of the play)

Dr Møller: Woman in her early thirties (at the start of the play)

SCENE 1

A lab, in a university nowhere in particular, in a time a handful of years away from the present day.

Dr Bach and Dr Møller conduct an experiment in which they look for the conditions which created the origin of life using a cloud chamber.

DR BACH: So, what are you having for dinner?

DR MØLLER: Fish pie.

DR BACH: I would kill for some fish and chips just now.

DR MØLLER: It's only 3pm? You ate two hours ago.

DR BACH: Doesn't mean I'm not starving.

Dr Møller straightens up in her chair.

DR MØLLER: Dr Bach, could you take a look at sample 2-28?

DR BACH: Doctor? You never use my title—

DR MØLLER: Now please.

DR BACH: Alright, alright. I'm doing it.

Dr Bach pulls up the file on her computer. A few keystrokes.

DR BACH: Wait... are those the disequilibrium levels?

DR MØLLER: Looks like it.
Methane and oxygen.

DR BACH: Methane? Are you sure there's not a leak in the chamber?

DR MØLLER: I'm checking everything now. I'm pretty sure—

    A beat.

It's the real thing, Bach.

DR BACH: I can't believe it. Metabolism.

    Beat.

Life. We've created life.

DR MØLLER: Could you run another sample from the chamber?

DR BACH: Yes, yes of course.

DR MØLLER: I'm going to call the ChemLab and ask if we can send over the sample.

Dr Møller picks up the lab phone and begins to dial.

DR BACH: I'll run these samples in a minute, um— loo
                run.

Dr Møller waves her off.

*Dr Bach leaves the lab. In the corridor outside, she pulls out
her phone and hits the speed dial.*

DR BACH: Isla, honey. You know that thing Mummy
                was working on? Well...

SCENE TWO

*Five years after the discovery. An anonymous park: with
swings, a slide and plenty of dark corners. Dr Bach and
Dr Møller inhabit one of these corners, they talk in muted
tones.*

DR BACH: Have you received your Creators payment
                for the month yet?

DR MØLLER: You mean my hush money?

DR BACH: It's not—

DR MØLLER: It really is. All of those contracts, all this
                secrecy.
                Don't tell me you're not even a little bit
                suspicious.

DR BACH: Okay fine.
                A little.
                But what are we supposed to do? It's not
                like we can unsign the damn contracts.

DR MØLLER: I refused my payment three months ago.
                Have been since.

DR BACH: What? How are you—

DR MØLLER: I have savings. Modest, but— they'll do for now.

DR BACH: Surely you don't think that will achieve anything.

DR MØLLER: It means I'm not associated with them anymore.

> *A beat.*

We should never have trusted them in the first place.

DR BACH: They haven't even done anything with our research—

DR MØLLER: Exactly. Doesn't that seem a bit strange to you?
Our discovery was ground-breaking. It should have been shared everywhere... and yet—
No research journal has published it, no media outlet has covered it—
No one knows anything about it. Why?

DR BACH: Corporate espionage? They're probably protecting their intellectual property—

Dr Møller exhales, exasperated.

DR BACH: When we sold them the results—
You were there. You felt the electricity in the room when they pitched.
Their visions, I really thought they'd create something—
Well, amazing.

DR MØLLER: This isn't about them making *the next iPhone,* Bach.

This is about the origins of life. Even if they did find a way to commercialise that—
Why haven't we had any communication from them besides payments in our bank accounts for five years?
Something— something is not right here.

DR BACH: Look, Møller, I don't know what you've been hearing.
But maybe a break from it all would help—
You seem... paranoid.

DR MØLLER: I cannot believe this.
Six years we practically lived in that lab together and now—

DR BACH: I only want to look out for you.

DR MØLLER: Then let's get to the bottom of this!
Together!

DR BACH: There is no bottom—

DR MØLLER: Why are you being so blind to what is right in front of you?

DR BACH: You have no evidence to back up what you're saying—

DR MØLLER: The absence of action is still evidence!

Beat.

DR BACH: I need to go pick Isla up.

DR MØLLER: Oh for fuck's—

DR BACH: You need anything, you just call me alright?

DR MØLLER: ... right.

SCENE THREE

20 years after the discovery was made. A rundown warehouse, dusty with disuse and littered with shards of glass. Both women sound more world weary, tired even.

DR MØLLER: Thank you for coming to meet me.

DR BACH: Of course. Though I was a bit surprised by the location.
An abandoned warehouse, really?

DR MØLLER: I had to make sure we weren't overheard.

DR BACH: Oh god, this isn't about—

DR MØLLER: What else?

DR BACH: It's too late now.
You know that, right?
They have too much power.

DR MØLLER: We still have to try.

DR BACH: They control half the working world—

DR MØLLER: Because of us.

DR BACH: We don't know that.

DR MØLLER: Don't we?
Twenty years ago we gave them the ability to create new life and now—

DR BACH: Not so loud!

DR MØLLER: No one is around, it's okay.

DR BACH: So what if they are? There's nothing to say it was our research that led them to—

DR MØLLER: The government buy out, the economic break down, the collapse of social life as we know it— it all only has one common

source Bach: the company we sold our
research to.

DR BACH: But how could they have orchestrated all of
that? All we gave them was the origin of
life—

DR MØLLER: Every crop they plant is invasive to the
point of strangling the native plants.
They achieved that because of us.
By using our research to rewrite the way
life can exist as we know it.
They control the food supply, Bach.
And with their grip on something so vital,
everything else just—

DR BACH: Falls into place.
God.

DR MØLLER: I think we're past gods now.

DR BACH: But—
What can *we* do?

DR MØLLER: Join us.

A beat.

DR BACH: Who is us?

DR MØLLER: The Resistance.

DR BACH: Fucking hell no. I've heard about you on the
radio, you guys— you're bad. Really bad.

DR MØLLER: And who controls the radio?

DR BACH: But the things you've been doing—

DR MØLLER: Accusations. Nothing more.

DR BACH: So the bomb in the town square—

DR MØLLER: A leaflet bomb.

DR BACH: The plane shot out of the sky?

DR MØLLER: Completely falsified.
Do you really think I would be part of something like that?
All we're doing is trying to correct the mismatch in knowledge.

DR BACH: Well—
Good luck, but I can't be involved.

A beat.

I have Isla to think about after all.

EPILOGUE

A town centre, 30 years after the discovery. An uncaring public stroll through, Dr Møller a single obstinate island among them.

DR MØLLER: Did you know that—

PERSON 1 : Sorry, not today.

DR MØLLER: My research shows that—

PERSON 2 : Listen lady, I just need to get to the bank so—

DR MØLLER: Cloud chambers have been around for years and the possibility of life within them—

DR BACH: Dr Møller?

DR MØLLER: Oh.
It's you.

DR BACH: Yes.
It's been a while.
How've you been keeping?

DR MØLLER: Peachy.
               How's Isla?

DR BACH: All grown up.

DR MØLLER: Right.
               I'm going to get back to the—

DR BACH: Can I—

                   Beat.

               Can I help?

DR MØLLER: What? I thought you said—

DR BACH: I know what I said.
               But, this is not the world I want for Isla.

DR MØLLER: You know they don't care, right? No one
               cares.

DR BACH: Yeah, I know how futile it feels to educate
               an uninterested audience.
               I lectured your undergrad class, remember?

                   A beat.

               But you're right, we have to try.

DR MØLLER: One cloud at a time?

DR BACH: One cloud at a time.

                   THE END.

PRIYANKA JHA is a Playwright and Director. She was bought up in Slough, the second daughter of Indian immigrants, and graduated from the University of Oxford with a degree in Philosophy, Politics and Economics. She is currently studying for a MLitt in Playwriting and Screenwriting at the University of St Andrews. Her work includes writing the short film 'I Contain Multitudes', produced by the Green Carnation Company for the Queer All About it monologue series, which featured as part of the program for Manchester's Turn On Fest in March 2021. Priyanka also writes for the stage and her short play 'Negative Space' will be performed at Hope Mill Theatre as part of Hive North's OutStageUs 2021. 'Chai for Sorrow; Chai for Joy', produced by Pier Productions for the BBC, will be Priyanka's directorial debut and her first time writing for radio. Currently, she is on the Traverse Young Writers program and is also working on a commission for Sanctuary Queer Arts.

From Priyanka: The insight, enthusiasm, and expertise Nanna bought to our sessions made creating this collaboration piece an absolute joy. I greatly enjoyed learning about Nanna's research, and found it was an interesting learning opportunity for me to understand more thoroughly both the work being done in the field of exoplanets and the importance of scientific literacy—which at its core is what this radio play sets out to explore. We also got to have chats about our mutual love of dragons and science fiction / fantasy literature, which was wonderful!

NANNA BACH MØLLER is a joint degree PhD student at the University of St Andrews and the University of Copenhagen. She is currently studying how clouds affect the chemistry of exoplanet atmospheres, and how prebiotic molecules (the precursors of life) might form in cloud droplets. She was born and raised in Denmark, just outside Copenhagen, and she has three degrees from the University of Copenhagen; a Bachelor's and Master's in physics, specializing in astrophysics, as well as a Bachelor's in biology, specializing in microbiology. Her research so far has been centred around exoplanets and astrobiology, and her main field of interest has been studying how life might be detected in exoplanet atmospheres based on its metabolism.

From Nanna: I was introduced to the StACES Anthology through my work with Emma Puranen, and I was intrigued by the collaboration. It has truly been a pleasure working with Priyanka, and I found her to be extremely skilled both as a writer and as a conversationalist. Through our conversations I felt like we got the chance to explore each other's fields in a way that was very eye-opening for me, and it has been fascinating to not only get an insight into a world very different from my own, but also see my own world interpreted through her writing.

Rise in Perfect Light

Writer: Maeghan Klinker
Researcher: Dr Aubrey Zerkle

Though my soul may set in darkness,
it will rise in perfect light;
I have loved the stars too fondly to be fearful of the night.
—Sarah Williams, 'The Old Astronomer to His Pupil'

In the dark of a sky I was not born under, the first star twinkles distantly. It pulses, as though it breathes. When I was a little girl and my grandmother was feeling indulgent, she used to tell us that all stars were a beating heart, the burning pulse of a universe that knew more of darkness than light. That if you listened carefully, you could hear them pounding their rhythm to the sky. I am as old now as my grandmother was then, and I know it to be fanciful nonsense, a story I repeat to my undergraduates with a self-conscious smile in an attempt to keep them interested in my kinetics of geochemical processes lecture. Lately, I find myself running over the story like a worry-stone, comforted by its familiar cadence though there are no undergraduates around to hear it.

A year ago, Centauri Interstellar University partnered with the Intergalactic Wayfarer Program to begin exploration of the Andromeda Galaxy. The department head at the university encouraged me to take a research sabbatical as a principal investigator on one of the terraforming projects, and I readily agreed. It seemed like a good idea at the time, a way to get back to my roots, to reacquaint myself with the search for knowledge that had driven me out among the stars. I could never have guessed then what I would learn.

I was stationed on a distant planet, officially Akhlys-X3295, known to everyone unlucky enough to live there simply as The Haze, a planet made of basalt and dust and purple sky. The station was the tiniest Wayfarer had, a consortium project of ten researchers and lab techs. All of us were desperate enough for discovery, for a claim to something larger than ourselves, to take whatever assignment Wayfarer would give us. Ona, the postdoc in my lab, used to grin during meals when we ate our bland, freeze-dried rations and whatever Khidir, the botanist, managed to eke from our greenhouse with its imported soil, and say that if our ambition could fill stomachs, we'd never be hungry again. But we were all starving for success, for something to make this indistinct landscape of dust and rock worth it. It was dangerous, that hunger. It made us bold. It made us desperate.

The Haze was not an inspiring place. Most days, I worried this planet held no secrets at all, but only dust and rock, and I would die shrouded in purple mist. The rocks weren't so bad, really, particularly as the principal investigator for the biogeochemistry arm of the Akhlys project, but it was the haze that drove me to madness. It distorted sound and light, muffling voices and turning everything blurry and indistinct so that we were constantly squinting. People became violet veiled ghosts and outcrops of boulders loomed like shadowed giants. As far as we could tell, there was no native life on Akhlys-X3295, though it's possible we just hadn't found it yet. The planet appeared to have had water once, before an impact event and a series of volcanic eruptions had led to drastic climactic change and the surface water had all dried up. We hadn't found proof of subterranean water, but its possibility was strongly hypothesized. We had been drilling for weeks pulling core samples from the ground, but so far it had been a lot of igneous flow and mafic minerals without a hint of fossilized remains to suggest the possibility of life.

The field site where Ona and I were pulling core samples that day was about as bland as anything The Haze had to offer. Visibility was low, and we were set up by a small outcropping of purple-red rock overlooking a flat, red expanse that blurred and disappeared into the purple mist. We were taking short cores with the robotic driller which had the name Darla affectionately scrawled in sharpie by one of the lab techs on a piece of fraying duct tape stuck to its battered outer shell. The drill—Darla—was supposed to do the hard work all on its own, but it wasn't exactly the newest piece of equipment and was given to fits of temper. I wasn't exactly the newest piece of equipment either, so I was supervising Darla while it ground and whirred its way deep into the rock and Ona prepped the other equipment we'd need to collect our initial field data.

We were pulling our second core when Darla started emitting a high-pitched whine, closely followed by a rattle and then a grinding that I could feel inside my skull as it started retracting its drill from the ground.

Ona cursed. 'Again?' she asked.

'We'll initiate a restart procedure after this core is pulled,' I said, trying to sound confident that turning Darla off and back on again was the answer to all our problems. Ona nodded dubiously.

When Darla had at last extracted the core and ceased its skull-numbing grating, I pulled the sample from the core barrel, fully expecting the same mafic rock rich in iron we'd been pulling all week. It was there, but so was something else. About halfway down a belt of some blue-green crystalline intrusion cut through the familiar red and black and grey rock. I traced my finger over it, then scratched at it lightly with a gloved finger of my envirosuit, testing its hardness. A thin layer of chalky dust came off beneath my nail.

'Ona, hand me the scratch kit please.'

Ona peered over my shoulder curiously as she handed me the kit and let out a low whistle when she saw what I was holding. 'Is that intrusion...glowing?' It almost looked that way. The blue-green mineral was refracting light strangely, though I wondered whether it didn't have as much to do with the way light travelled through the dense haze of the atmosphere as with the mineral itself. I hummed noncommittedly while digging around in the kit, and removed a piece of talc. I scraped it lightly against the blue-green bar. It left a small scratch across the surface. I dug at it harder, and a dusting of powder drifted down to my palm.

'Softer than talc?' Ona asked incredulously. 'In all this?' She gestured broadly to the flat expanse that had yielded nothing but igneous rock and hard iron-based minerals.

'Let's pull a few more samples from around here and get it back to the lab,' I said. My pulse thrummed excitedly in my veins. Maybe The Haze was keeping secrets after all.

* * *

Khidir was tending his plants outside the research station when we got back. They were mostly sad-looking things with deep red leaves that were nearly black, and which hung limply from drunkenly listing stalks. Khidir waved as we approached.

'Find anything good today?' He asked. It was half a joke; he knew we hadn't found anything exciting for weeks.

Ona grinned wildly. 'Wait until you see.'

It was all anyone could talk about at dinner. It was certainly more interesting than our rehydrated peas. We weren't even sure what it was yet. We hypothesized it was an undiscovered mineral, something unique to Akhlys-X3295.

Sometimes the truth is more improbable than any hypothesis.

It wasn't until I ran a portion of the sample through the x-ray diffractometer that we realized it was organic. It wasn't until Ona tried to test its dissolution rate that we realized it was still alive.

'Alive?' I said sceptically, 'Cutting through the rock like that? It didn't look like a bedding plane.'

'Maybe it wasn't really cutting through,' Ona said slowly, 'maybe it was surrounded later, in the flow event.'

'You think it could withstand that kind of heat?'

'Who knows what's possible?' she asked. There was awe and excitement in her voice. The thrill of discovery. There was more to discover still.

According to Dante, our biologist, it was some tardigrade-like creature, capable of withstanding extreme conditions, even dehydrating itself and remaining in torpor for an as-yet-indeterminate time. We'd accidentally rehydrated it when trying to study its dissolution rate, and now the alien creatures appeared to be bioluminescent, flickering and flashing in little blue-green specks visible individually only under a microscope. But they didn't move individually. They appeared to form little colonies, joining together to move in tandem, creating complex patterns as they flashed and swirled in their petri dishes. Sometimes, in the evening, we would turn off all the lights in the lab and gather together to watch our own personal alien light show. But we gradually realized the creatures were slow and lethargic. We assumed it was because they hadn't evolved for the regulated atmosphere of the research station. They belonged in The Haze.

So began our experiments.

Our first trial yielded surprising results. When exposed to low concentrations of Akhlys's atmosphere, the bioluminescence of the alien creatures flared dramatically and they began vibrating excitedly, quivering together. They were so bright, and their movements so coordinated, that they appeared to grow in size, transforming from many tiny specks of light into a collection of small glowing orbs. It was unlike anything I had ever seen.

Gradually, we increased the concentration of atmosphere until our sixteenth trial, when we took the creatures out into The Haze. It wasn't laboratory conditions, but some things can't be discovered in a lab. Certainly not this, at any rate.

When the lids of the petri dishes were removed and the alien creatures were exposed to The Haze, their bioluminescence flared brilliantly and they began to swarm into the air, swirling together like blue-green embers from a bonfire. I don't think any of us believed it at first. We stood staring stupidly. It wasn't until The Haze began to shift around them, thickening until we could make out indistinct shapes forming and unravelling in the purple mist that we realized they were capable of more than we anticipated. The mist-forms were tall and gaunt, and in the middle of their chests, the blue-green creatures gathered together, swirling and pulsing like a beating heart. Each had three pairs of limbs, though some stood on only four or two of the slim appendages, and their graceful necks arched serpentine above us leading to flat, featureless faces.

I don't think they meant to scare us, though at the time I hardly considered them capable of that level of thought. Three of the mist-forms moved forward at the same time. Someone shouted, and we surged backwards, stumbling for the safety of the research station. Khidir tripped and fell over one of the damn red rocks that littered practically every inch of the ground. There must have been a flaw in his envirosuit, or maybe it was just bad luck, but when Khidir hit the ground his suit tore along the arm. This in itself was not terrible. Humans could survive in the atmosphere of The Haze for a few hours before side-effects began to set in. It was what happened next that was concerning. One of the mist-forms reached for him. Not just for him, but for the tear in his suit.

When it touched his arm he gasped, and a blue-green streak like lightning shot along his veins. Dante turned back and pulled Khidir up, and we stumbled into the station then sealed the door tightly behind us. We took Khidir to the med bay and put him in isolation. Protocol demanded it for any exposure to alien lifeforms or in cases of an envirosuit breach. In reality, we were all thinking of that blue-green lightning along his veins. We didn't know what it could mean, what it would do.

We would learn.

* * *

The plants in Khidir's garden outside the station thrived. Their stalks no longer listed drunkenly but grew tall and proud. Their deep red-black leaves spread broadly outward, absorbing as much of the meagre light as they could. We thought it had something to do with the creatures or their mist-forms. In a way we were right, but not as we expected.

It had been a few days since Khidir was released from isolation. He hadn't shown any side-effects from the interaction with the mist-form and said he felt fine. More than fine. He was the first to venture back outside, despite our protests. He said he needed to check on his plants, that he didn't think the creatures were violent. We instituted a buddy system for anyone going outside, and Dante accompanied him. They reported that the mist-forms kept back from the station. The creatures did not try to approach nor show any signs of aggression. Slowly, we began venturing out again. The mist-forms kept their distance, forming and dissolving in the haze so they seemed no more than hallucinations, the blue-green glowing creatures at their hearts fading in and out like will-o-the-wisps.

I was accompanying Khidir while he tended his plants when I first noticed the hole in his envirosuit. We'd disposed of the old one, but this one had a long thin slice along the upper arm, facing in towards his body so that it wasn't ordinarily visible. It was a clean cut. Precise. Intentional.

'Khidir,' I said carefully, 'there is a hole in your suit.' It felt stupid to say. Redundant. I was quite confident both of us knew it was there, but all scientific enquiry starts with observation, even of something obvious. It was a question unformed, an accusation not yet made.

Khidir looked solemnly up at me from where he knelt inspecting a tender pair of leaves pushing their way through the red ground. 'Don't worry, Atsuko. I'm okay. It's all okay. I understand them better this way.'

I frowned down at him. 'What are you talking about?' I looked at Khidir more closely, noticing the way his veins stood out against his brown skin, a more vibrant shade of blue than normal. 'Khidir, I think we ought to get Dante to take a look at you. Let's go back inside.'

Khidir shook his head. 'No, just listen. I *understand* now. When that creature touched me, it—it communicated with me. It showed me what the plants needed, all the connections I was missing.' He smiled and gestured with his pruning shears at his little plot of ground, previously a sad patch of dirt where plants went to die and now flourishing with oddly coloured vegetation.

'So, the aliens are...talking to you...through the haze,' I said, gesturing towards the tear in his suit. I wanted to make sure I had the facts straight for the report I was surely going to have to make later. It sounded unhinged. I thought it was a delayed onset of side effects from his accident or that he was delusional from too much exposure to Akhly's atmosphere. But part of me wondered. After all, we'd pulled aliens from the ground and brought them back to life. I heard Ona's voice in my head, asking me who knew what was possible. But most damning of all, I wanted it to be true.

'They know so much,' he said, voice filled with wonder. 'They help me understand.' He held my gaze, unwavering. 'You could understand too.'

We walked as far from the research station as we could without losing sight of it. The nearest mist-form hovered on the edge of visibility. When we were close enough to the creatures that the blue-green light ghosted over our faces, we paused.

'Give me your hand,' Khidir said. I don't know what I was expecting. Not that. Not what came after. I gave him my hand. The mist-form hovered close by, unmoving. It felt like it was watching us. Delicately, clinically, he sliced through the arm of my envirosuit with his pruning shears. A clean slice down the forearm, exposing my skin. I do not remember being afraid. A sense of anticipation hummed through me. Curiosity. A hunger I could not name. The mist-form unravelled and reformed mere inches away, the blue-green light of the creatures snaking through the air like lightning. I would have pulled away, stumbled back, but Khidir's grip on my arm kept me grounded. Gently, the mist-form unfurled a tendril and tenderly brushed against my skin like a breath of air. I gasped. For one scintillating moment I *understood*. Everything made perfect sense. I heard millions of voices, saw flashes from millions of lives. For one shining moment, I contained all of reality within me. Then it faded and I was left with just one truth: the creatures understood more than we had yet chanced to discover.

'Oh,' I sighed. I could hear the awe in my voice as I said it.

The thrill of discovery. The weight of knowledge. 'There's so much still for us to learn.'

I started sneaking out after that. Khidir did too. Or perhaps he had been sneaking out since his accident. I do not know. We didn't speak of it, but we both knew the other was going out into the mist, seeking the creatures and their knowledge. We didn't tell the others. Not at first.

Night after night, I chased the blue-green lights out into The Haze, searching for answers to questions I didn't know how to ask. The creatures showed me Akhlys and all that it had been. How once, the creatures had thrived, forming complex structures like coral reefs when they lay dormant and chasing each other through the air in streaks of blue-green light when they were not. They showed me how they manipulated the mist to create the mist-forms and what Khidir's plants had needed to flourish in Akhlys's soil. I saw the impact event that had caused the planet's surface water to dry up and the formation of caves deep underground that still held vestiges of water. But the creatures' knowledge was not limited to Akhlys. It seemed no corner of the universe was unknown to them.

They sought perfect understanding. They believed in a Truth at the heart of the universe and strove to find it. Perhaps it was driven by their shared consciousness, a kind of hive mind that allowed them to share thoughts and experiences. They thought if they could understand existence, they would grasp the Truth. I do not know what they hoped to do after that. Maybe they only wanted to understand. It was a desire I knew well.

I was slipping out for one of my nightly visits when Ona caught me. I admit, I am old now and not as stealthy as I once was. She must have seen me leaving and followed me out. Either way, I was deep in the midnight mist when I heard her call my name. I froze, thinking it a trick of The Haze. From the shadowed mists, a figure emerged tinged with blue-green light, drawn by the sound of her shouting. My brain struggled to reconcile what I was looking at with the figure I recognized.

It was Khidir.

'Are you alright?' he asked. The shock must have registered on my face. I nodded, unable to speak. His veins were glowing. Not in a subtle way. Glowing like someone had pumped his bloodstream full of fluorescent dye. I glanced to the skin of my forearm. My own veins held a softer glow, so thin that I could easily convince myself it was not there if I did not have Khidir beside me as living proof of what I would become.

'Atsuko!' Ona called again.

Khidir and I both jerked our heads at the sound as Ona came stumbling up out of the mist.

'Atsuko,' she repeated, sounding relieved. Then, 'Khidir?' She looked between us as if trying to pull answers from the air, but it was too shrouded in the obscurity of The Haze to help her. 'What's going on?'

Khidir and I shared an uneasy look. I do not remember exactly how we told her, only that I cannot forget the look on her face when she said, 'show me,' or how, for a moment, when the mist-form brushed against Ona's skin, I thought I saw something pass through her eyes, an unfamiliar galaxy or an exploding star, but it was gone just as quickly.

Ona inhaled sharply and stumbled back as the mist-form retreated. Khidir held out a hand to steady her. 'I *saw*,' she gasped, 'For a moment I saw everything all at once.' There was a hunger to her words. A boldness. A desperation. 'I want to know; I want to know everything.'

But knowledge never comes freely. There is always a price.

* * *

Khidir was the first to pay it. Of the three of us, he had had the most time to consider it. It was becoming impossible to hide the physical changes, the way his veins fluoresced when he was out in The Haze, or how his eyes reflected galaxies beyond the one we inhabited. Soon, the others would notice. So he made his decision. The creatures had made us all the same offer: an invitation to join the collective consciousness, a chance at obtaining perfect knowledge. It sounds absurd to say it, as though I am reciting one of my grandmother's stories. But I was there. I saw it happen.

Khidir was waiting for me outside the station. Ona held his hand. 'I want to understand,' he said, and I nodded. I took his other hand and together we walked out into the mist. It did not take us long to find one of the mist-forms. It was smaller than the others, but the creatures at its heart shone bright as a supernova. Khidir dropped our hands and slipped from his envirosuit, so he stood only in his standard issue Wayfarer t-shirt and loose grey bottoms. His veins shone brilliantly as his skin met Akhlys's atmosphere. He breathed in deeply and when he opened his eyes they shone with the light of a distant nebula.

The mist-form moved in a serpentine fashion, dissolving and reforming, drifting along the ground like liquid smoke while the creatures bobbed slowly forward in an orb of blue-green light. Slowly, the mist-form coalesced in front of Khidir, slim and elegant, two pairs of limbs hanging loosely at its side. Khidir turned and looked at us. 'I'm sorry,' he said. 'I don't know what you should tell the others. But you understand, don't you? I need to know.' I recognized the hunger in his voice. It echoed the one curling itself in my own chest. We nodded. We did not know how to say goodbye, or whether it was a goodbye at all, and so we said nothing. The mist thickened and swirled, embracing him. He took a step forward, and then another. Ona and I watched until he disappeared into The Haze. He did not look back.

In the end, we kept our silence and said nothing to the others. It was not a decision made lightly. I argued that we had come here to discover and to learn, but that such discovery was meaningless if we did not share our knowledge. But Ona was afraid if we told the others that they would stop us from speaking with the creatures, that we might get sent back to Centauri University before we had fully understood. Despite my arguments, I found I could not bear the possibility of being forced away before I had discovered all that I could. So we helped with the search party, spent days wandering around The Haze searching for a trace of Khidir that we knew we would not find. I have never felt so ashamed.

Dante, I did not want to lie to you. I have spent my life devoted to the pursuit of knowledge, to uncovering the truth and sharing it. That is why, at first, I could not take the creatures' offer.

As my fellow researchers on Akhlys, you will know this report is not my best work. I am too close to the study, too involved as a subject to reliably speak with objectivity. I only hope that one of you will find this before long, so you will understand. That is why we came here, isn't it? To understand. I have learned more these past few months than in a lifetime of study, and I have written my account so that you may share it. In my notebooks, on my desk, you will find all the data I collected from the creatures, all the knowledge I could gather and record. I want you to know you need not mourn. It was our decision in the end, a choice we made freely. Perhaps you will not think it safe to continue our study of Akhlys, or maybe Wayfarer will shut the project down. Maybe you will sign nondisclosure statements and be sworn to secrecy, and no one else will read this report and know what truly happened here. Or maybe you will seek perfect understanding. Perhaps you will join us. It is your choice, just as it was mine.

Ona was the one that convinced me in the end, or maybe it was the creatures speaking through her. She was ready to walk into The Haze as Khidir had, ready to seek perfect understanding. She turned before the mist swallowed her.

'Oh, Atsuko,' she said, breathless, 'look at what we've discovered, all that we can discover still.' Her eyes reflected galaxies I could not see. 'It's beautiful,' she murmured, 'if you only knew.' She held out her hand. 'You could know,' she said. 'You could understand.'

I couldn't pull my eyes from hers and the stars I saw there. Already, my veins glowed as blue as Cherenkov radiation, as a blue gas giant, as the sky I was born under and now can only distantly remember. I could feel my pulse in the stars, a vein of light through the immense darkness, an endlessness waiting to embrace me. It is there, hovering at the edge of my consciousness. The answer to every question I have ever asked, answers to questions I haven't yet thought of asking. But I let her walk into the mist alone. There was still one thing left for me to do. This letter. This report. This confession. Call it what you will. It will be easy, now that my task is done, my experience shared, for me to follow her into The Haze.

Knowledge wells within me, and I rise in perfect light.

In the dark of a sky I was not born under, the first star twinkles distantly. It pulses, and I feel it breathe.

MAEGHAN KLINKER is a postgraduate student studying Medieval English at the University of St Andrews, where she spends her time reading old books and brushing the dust off of stories. When she's not stumbling over medieval texts, she spends her time reading sci-fi and fantasy books in Modern English, writing stories, talking to the trees, and going on walks with her dog. Confronted with infinite knowledge and only one question that can be answered, she would like to know: if the universe is expanding, what is it expanding into?

From Maeghan: Collaborating with Aubrey was a wonderful experience that provided vivid details and inspiration for my story. From sharing her opinion on the most boring kind of rock, to the struggles of conducting research in cave systems, and the types of equipment found in a lab, Aubrey's research and experience was invaluable to the creation of Akhlys and the researchers that live there. While some of the details didn't make it into the final version, all of them provided an insight into the life and drive of a researcher that helped flesh out the story. This collaboration was an awesome opportunity and learning experience that really highlighted how science and art can build off one another to create something compelling.

DR AUBREY ZERKLE is a biogeochemist and Reader in the School of Earth & Environmental Sciences at the University of St Andrews. Aubrey uses an inter-disciplinary approach, combining stable isotope geochemistry and microbiology, to probe the development of early life on Earth, and to devise methods for recognizing microbial life outside our planet.

From Aubrey: During the Anthology collaboration, I particularly enjoyed exploring society's broader fascination with exoplanet science, as seen through a non-scientist's eyes. I found it invigorating to explore my own creativity during the brainstorming process, and to see ideas brought to life in Maeghan's highly descriptive prose.

A Momentary Brightening

Writer: Laura Muetzelfeldt
Researcher: Dr Martin Dominik

Karl awoke to the shuttered darkness in time for dinner. After checking all the lights were off, he raised the blind. The sky was darkening, and the first stars of the cloudless Chilean night were visible—Scorpius and the Southern Cross. Orion was starting to set. From his window in the accommodation block he could see a couple of the many domes that were dotted along the mountain ridge. Like watchtowers, he'd thought, as he arrived at the at the gates of the European Southern Observatory yesterday. The setting sun illuminated the buildings, their massive domes lilac in the fading light.

He stretched, heard his neck crunch, and checked his watch even though he knew it was too late to call Joshua. La Silla was five hours behind home—Grandpa would have already put him to bed.

Maybe tomorrow he'd be able to tell Joshua he'd found a new planet. The thought made him suddenly hungry. Karl remembered a conversation they'd had in the park about his research—the first time they discussed gravitational lensing: 'It's when the gravity from the nearer star bends the light from the far away one,' Karl explained. 'It works like the bottom of a wine glass, so the far away star gets brighter.' Joshua was sitting on a stationary swing, head tilted to one side, listening.

There was movement now in the apartment above. Another astronomer getting up just as darkness fell. Footsteps heading towards the bathroom, the faint sound of a tap running.

'Sounds like an upside-down place,' his son had said, when they chatted this morning.

He'd reasoned with him—*no, we are just nocturnal.* But Karl had the feeling now, as he got ready for work in the early evening, of something being flipped. Here, Orion stands on its head, not like in the Northern Hemisphere.

Karl closed the blind and the curtains as the sky darkened to an inky blue. It was only then he turned on the light, careful to do his bit to ensure zero light pollution. Another glance at his watch, then he pulled on the trousers, shirt, and jumper that he'd hung over the back of a chair, smoothing out the creases in the trousers with his hands.

In the bathroom, there was only the most cursory glance in the mirror before he reached for his shaving brush. His brown curly hair badly needed a cut. Karl pushed his dark-rimmed glasses back up to the bridge of his nose to the groove that had been worn there.

Grabbing the shaving soap, he worked up a lather. At their flat in Edinburgh, Joshua always stood beside him when he shaved. Looking into the unfamiliar mirror, Karl started shaving in the same methodical way he always did, starting by his left ear. He imagined Joshua beside him, jutting out his chin, drawing the back of a comb over his too-soft skin. A silly face, like his, when Joshua pretended to shave under the nose, top lip stretched down over his front teeth. At the end, his son would push out his chin again, rub the skin on his neck like he'd seen him do.

'Missed a bit,' Karl said the last time they stood like this. Then, the flash of a smile before Joshua resumed the same serious expression that was now familiar. Karl worried that this smile was just a momentary brightness, a one-time event, never to be repeated.

He imagined ruffling his son's hair. '*Dad,*' Joshua would say, scowling at him. Joshua was Sofie when he was angry—his face and her face were the same. It wasn't supposed to be just the two of them. He felt guilty leaving him, but he had to work.

When Sofie died he'd worried that there would be no more laughter. He looked out through the open bathroom door and saw the photo he'd brought with him of the three of them at Portobello Beach. Sofie was tickling Joshua, his face alight with laughter. In a few months it would be spring again—a whole year since she passed. At first her only symptoms were hiccups and being confused, but the second stroke was fatal. It happened so quickly that it didn't seem real. At the hospital, he wanted to argue, *but she had none of the risk factors*, to appeal to one of the doctors. But she was still gone.

Sofie made him normal. She'd found him funny—no one else did. Without her, he was just an astrophysicist with few friends. When she was in the house, there was always a radio turned up too loud in the room she was no longer in. It had annoyed him at the time; it seemed like he was always turning radios off. Now the house was too quiet. He remembered her dancing to Bowie in the kitchen, making him dance. She'd just run 10k. The skin on her neck was salty when he kissed her. He cleared his throat, blinked away the memory.

A dark emptiness opened up inside him, a luxury he didn't allow himself when he was at home. Karl saw how his son withdrew, how he played alone, not with other children. He couldn't reach him. All Karl could do was keep going, not knowing what else to do. At least he had his work.

Okay, he said to himself, let's do this. When he shouldered his work bag, a queasiness started, mixed with anticipation. There was the feeling of wasting time, the pressure to make the most of the opportunity of being here, at La Silla. One session of the week he'd been awarded was already gone. He strode towards the door, bent to tie his laces, cataloguing, as he liked to, the aches and pains—new and returning. The ball of his hip bone on the right side, sometimes an uncomfortable ache, today was just *there*. The knotted shoulder muscles. The crunch in his neck when he straightened up again.

With a torch held in his mouth, he switched off the light, stepped through the first door, then the next, into the beautifully imperfect darkness.

The skies in Chile were nothing like at home. He looked up and thought again—how could you not?—that he'd been lied to all his life. There were more stars than seemed possible. There was the Milky Way—thousands of the hundreds of billions of stars visible, dark cloud constellations stretching like shadows at the centre. In the dark shapes, he recognised the Mother Llama, the Baby Llama, the Toad. He stared, mouth open, heart beating. So many stars! He tilted his head all the way back. So much sky!

His eyes then searched, as they always did, for Ursa Minor and Kochab, before berating himself—you can't see Kochab in the Southern Hemisphere. He'd never told anyone that he thought he saw this star brighten after Sofie died. It couldn't, he reasoned, yet he saw it with his own eyes. That lie parents tell children, he thought, that a dead loved one is a star watching over them. He shook his head; did a small part of him want to be lied to like a child?

He tilted his head back again and inhaled the dry, baked smell of the earth. The warmth of the sun was still in the ground, even at the top of the mountain, and he had an urge to take his shoes and socks off, feel the memory of the heat.

Unlike the stopover in Santiago, there was no noise—no traffic, no sirens, no voices, not even cicadas. It was only his second day, but he was starting to enjoy the silence. He yawned again, waiting for the instant coffee to start working, the bitter taste still in his mouth. A glance at his watch. There was plenty time to grab some food from the cafeteria before his session was due to start.

He'd just sat down and taken a few bites of stew when a tall, skinny man waved and bounded towards him from the other side of the cafeteria—Niels, a Danish PhD student who he'd invited to join him this week. They'd been in touch using Zoom because of their shared research interests, and to arrange this visit, but yesterday was the first time they'd met in person; last night was their first shift together.

Karl raised his hand, returning the wave. He liked Niels but, as always, was looking forward to a few more minutes by himself.

'Professor.'

'Niels,' said Karl, nodding.

The man sat down in the chair opposite and stared at him, shiny-eyed, foot tapping, unable to keep still.

Karl stared back, brow creased.

'So you haven't heard?' Niels said, pushing his sun-bleached hair from his eyes, his eyelashes white against his tanned skin.

Karl put down his knife and fork.

'Last night the American team at Cerro Tololo saw a lensing effect on the same star,' he paused, '*twice*.'

Niels watched this news settle on Karl's face, a mixture of confusion and disbelief. It was a few seconds before Karl composed himself.

'Twice?' He scratched his neck. 'You're sure?'

'Yes, saw the data myself,' Niels said, tapping his foot so energetically that his whole body vibrated.

'Both events achromatic?' Karl asked.

'Yes, all wavelengths.'

'It can't be,' Karl said, hand rubbing the smooth skin on his neck.

'You yourself told me scientists shouldn't use the word *can't*,' Niels said.

The two men looked at each other. It was Karl who broke the tension, smiled first. Then both men laughed.

Karl remembered another conversation he had with Joshua about gravitational lensing one dinnertime. What had Joshua said? Something like, *could something use this to send us a message from space, like Morse code?*

'Even if they knew Morse code...' Karl replied, then saw the brightness in his son's eyes dim. He understood the need to believe in impossible things.

'But I suppose, if they *could* move something with at least the mass of an asteroid,' Karl continued, 'if they attached some method of propulsion, then...why not?'

Joshua dropped his fork. It clinked off the plate and baked beans landed in a little constellation on the tablecloth.

'Cool,' was all he said, the bright spark back in his eyes. He was quiet for a bit, that same look Sofie had when she was turning something over in her mind.

'So not Morse code,' Joshua said.

'Highly unlikely.'

Joshua mopped up the last of the sauce with a square of toast.

'What then?'

'Well, that's the question.'

Karl and Niels left the cafeteria together, stepping out into the mountain air, their dim torches pointed at the ground. It was a short walk to the control room building but coats were necessary in the evening. As before, Niels chatted with the kind of confidence that Karl had assumed was the result of a private education, though it turned out not to be. Last night when they walked the same path, Karl worried that Niels would talk too much, but this proved groundless; at work, Niels was totally focused and silent unless there was a reason to speak.

In the control room, Karl spoke to Antonia, the telescope engineer he'd been assigned for the night. Her dark-brown hair was scraped back into a ponytail, and she wasn't wearing make up, he noted, approvingly. Sofie always used to wear her hair like that when she was going for a run. He missed the ordinariness of that, her preparations—stretching, picking a playlist on her phone, plugging in headphones—before heading out the door, letting it bang.

Now, something else was mixed with the empty sadness of this. Guilt? Karl looked down at the papers he was holding, away from Antonia's brown eyes. He hadn't expected to notice women again so soon. It was an unwanted complication; he preferred the simple companionship of grief.

When he resumed speaking, Antonia nodded, listening carefully to his instructions. The plan had changed—he wanted to look at the same star that the American team had been observing last night. It would take a few moments to set up, Antonia told him, her ponytail bobbing as she walked to a desk on the other side of the room.

Turning his back on her, Karl opened his laptop and accessed the data from the American team. He called to Niels in a voice that he just recognised.

'You're right. The light curve is the same. Same magnitude.' Karl said. A little spark flickered in his eyes.

'Star NWS2021/dqb,' said Niels.

'Yes, exactly.'

Karl shook his head, eyes wide.

To observe the same star brightening due to lensing *twice*, well, it had never happened before. They thought it was impossible.

He searched for a scientific reason. There had to be one.

But another thought rose up. What if there *is* somebody out there? What if they are trying to communicate with us? His head felt light.

Antonia smiled at him across the room. Had he been looking at her without realising? Karl felt the warmth as his face coloured. The last time he met Sofie's mum, she had put a hand on his arm and urged, *don't shut yourself away, she'd want you to find someone else.* But, still, even a smile felt like betrayal. Quickly, he turned to look at Niels.

'The talk is of going back through the data,' Niels called over.

'But we've never found anything like this before,' Karl said.

'We weren't looking then.' Niels smiled.

Karl turned to face the monitor. His head ran simulations. The only thing that could cause this effect was a massive object, a star, a planet... Or an asteroid, yes. The only criterion was that the foreground object needs to be massive and the observed background star needs to be small. Karl ran his hand over his chin, down his neck. Ever since Einstein theorised about lensing, it was understood to be a one-time achromatic event, a momentary brightening. The alignment couldn't happen more than once.

Only it could.

The hair on the back of his neck stood up. He didn't know what to do with his hands. They felt heavy, light. He stuffed them in his pockets.

His mind explored the possibilities. And if there was another brightening, then what? *Might* they observe a pattern?

Karl fixed his eyes on the star as it flickered on the monitor in front of him—the live feed now up and running. People use the word 'twinkling', but this doesn't describe the way the light…

But he didn't complete this thought.

He stared. There on the screen. It couldn't be. His pulse quickened.

The star seemed to be getting closer, the brightness increasing. He stared at the monitor, a full feeling in his chest.

Was he imagining it? Was it brighter?

Niels shouted from the other side of the room: 'It's happening again!'

'I…' Karl opened his mouth, but no words came. He sat there staring at the monitor, mouth open.

'Less time between the peaks but the same brightness curve,' Niels said, his voice still raised.

Karl stood up, walked towards Niels. He'd gone over to shake his hand, but Niels opened his arms wide, inviting a hug. Karl patted him twice on the back before releasing. Antonia stood beside him, and there was an awkward hug between them too—she was bony and he could smell her shampoo.

They grinned at each other. They were all part of something; it connected them. Like being in the Launch Control Center in Florida just after a shuttle launch, he supposed.

This is it, Karl thought, the discovery he'd been waiting for. Something we don't have an explanation for. The feeling was humbling, thrilling, liberating. Soon, he'd be able to tell Joshua. He imagined telling Sofie. She used to be the first person he wanted to tell when something like this happened. He turned away from the others, closed his eyes, and tried to picture her, to hear what she might say.

An hour before sunrise they shut down the computers, said goodbye to Antonia and thanked her for her help. As they left, she held the door for them.

'See you later,' she said.

Karl looked back at her, a line forming between his eyebrows.

'I'm your engineer again tonight,' she explained, her brown eyes smiling.

He held her gaze for a second, then looked away, trying to hide his smile.

Karl knew sleep would not be forthcoming, so he went to the cafeteria with Niels, sat at a table with a few others and shared what they found, feeling part of something bigger. As the morning continued, more astronomers joined them, and the time passed quickly in conversation, all of their voices animated, like children.

Soon it was time to call his son.

It rang several times, and he worried he'd miscalculated the time difference. But, just as he was about to hang up, someone answered.

'Joshua?'

'Dad?'

'Son, we found it,' said Karl, his voice cracking.

'What?'

'The same star brightening. Three times so far.'

There was a pause.

'But that's...'

'Not anymore.'

Another pause. Karl smiled and knew Joshua was smiling as well, his face alight.

'So, what do you think it is?' Joshua asked, eventually.

'What do *you* think it is? Something like this can't happen by chance,' Karl said.

'So now we just have to find the pattern, crack the code,' Joshua said.

'Find out what they are trying to say,' Karl agreed.

A silence stretched, full of possibility.

LAURA MUETZELFELDT is a writer from Glasgow who has been published in journals such as *The International Literary Quarterly* and short story collections like *New Writing Scotland*. Laura completed an MLitt in Creative Writing at the University of Glasgow and is currently a Creative Writing PhD student at the University of St Andrews.

From Laura: I feel incredibly lucky to have been involved with this project and to have been allowed a small glimpse into Martin's research. His enthusiasm for his work was contagious and, ultimately, inspiring. Writing is often a solitary pursuit and I found the process of planning and writing this story both challenging and thrilling. Martin's ideas and feedback was essential in shaping the story and, based on this wholly positive experience, I am actively seeking similar opportunities to collaborate on creative work in the future.

DR MARTIN DOMINIK is a Reader in Physics & Astronomy at the University of St Andrews. Since 1993, his research has focused on applications of the gravitational bending of light, and in particular its potential for obtaining the demographics of planets throughout the Milky Way. He organised a Royal Society Discussion Meeting on "The detection of extra-terrestrial life and the consequences for science and society" and designed an exhibit "What does it mean to be human?" on the Search for Extra-Terrestrial Intelligence. Martin is also President of the Network of Researchers on the Chemical Evolution of Life (NoRCEL), as well as a strong advocate of communication being an essential part of science, and science being an integral part of society and culture.

From Martin: I could not resist telling a long story in our meetings involving the diversity of planets and planetary systems, the emergence of life and the potential universality of biology, the co-evolution of life with its environment, the enshrined memory of evolution in DNA, the failure of anthropocentric views, and speculations about unknown chemistry of potentially stable heavy elements. By just letting the mind flow, some new thoughts were triggered through this interaction. Apparently, imagination stands at the beginning of the process of scientific enquiry, and the advancement of human knowledge is guided by questions. To most of them none of us has an answer...yet.

After Colour

Writer: Kiale Palpant
Researcher: Oliver Herbort

'Our eyes adjust to the dark.'
—Tracy K. Smith

Tom sat at the table, bowl and cup placed upside down in front of him, the window closed. He felt the dust settling onto his jeans again, the soot soaking into his skin, into his mask, beneath his finger nails, somehow staying beneath his eyelids even when he kept them closed for hours on end. Tom walked over to the window, where the dark clouds let slip a ray of white light, stopping their chokehold on the sun for a moment.

The storm sat on the horizon, pencil stroke lines showing him where it fell. He waited by the window as the clouds wandered across the sky, darkening the shadows of blighted grass and lonely men, waiting for the tempest to drop soot from the sky.

His makeshift air filtration system was locked into all the openings in the house. He'd done that hours ago. At breakfast, he'd taken a round of the house and checked all the plastic covering the walls and windows, duct taping any cracks that had emerged at the edges, dusting the ash off surfaces until the cloth in his hand grew too dirty to clean anything.

The clouds came quickly, suffocating the rest of the light in the pencilled world. Tom propped his hat on his head and pulled a rocking chair up to the window. He'd watched the storms too often to find them interesting anymore. He knew as soon as those clouds hit, his world would go dark, the wind tossing up the soot on the ground and stirring it up into a frenzy until wind and cloud and graphite rain scratched out whatever remained.

The rocking chair felt comfortable now, his body rocking to the rhythm of the wind outside, feeling the house rocking with him, and the wind and the storm raging against them all.

He clicked on the old television set he'd inherited from his father and waited as the opening credits of *It's a Wonderful Life* flicked across the screen one after the other until it all went black. The night sky appeared on the glass, hundreds of pixelated white stars blinking at him from across the room, prayers echoing around the heavens that were clear and bright and clean.

Looks like we'll have to send someone down, the voice in heaven was saying. And the other responding, *George Bailey...Yes, tonight's his crucial night.* And good faithful Clarence rushing into the sky, hoping to get his wings.

Now, keep your eyes open, said the voices, and the screen became a blur of fog.

The screen matched Tom's own window, now a swirl of indiscernible grey.

Keep your eyes open. As if there were something to see, something to keep his attention, something important. But all Tom saw were the clouds piling in upon him, the flashing TV screen the only light in the room. A mug of coffee and a plate of cold eggs sat on the table, their shadows playing against the wall as the screen flashed through its images. The lights seemed to mock the framed newspaper clipping his dad had hung there long ago, the one that announced the storms, the masks, the new air-filtration homes, and the way the ash would blind humanity.

It was also so long ago that his father had sat him down on the porch, under the dusty skies, and told him about the time in his childhood when he had gone fishing. Tom had learned to imagine a liquid as clear as glass, gallons of it pouring through the dirt, and, in the glass, animals with skin like diamonds that you could catch with a stick and a string and a fly made out of thread and metal. He had imagined it again and again, especially when his father would make him a rod out of stick and string and teach him how to cast off the back porch into the dust.

But he had never been able to imagine the colours. His father said that the world used to have a vibrancy, that our eyes long ago could see more of the world. Like the colour green, the colour of life and of things called plants, leaves, trees, grass, ocean. And blue, red, yellow that left when the sun did, magenta, indigo, and lavender. A whole realm of light Tom could not understand, would never be able to see.

Jimmy Stewart stared out at him from the screen. Tom liked that George Bailey lived in a world like his, a black and white man in a black and white city. He felt on level ground with a man like that. You could trust a man who saw things the same as you, you could believe what he said.

In the television, George Bailey stood looking off the bridge maniacally, desperately, letting the snow fall on his head when Tom heard three taps on the door. Then three more. He looked away and the room was dark, the wind still engaged in its fist fight with the sky.

Three short taps again.

He fixed his hat on his head and stood slowly, a stiff grunt escaping his throat as he pushed himself out of the chair.

Tom walked over to the heavy metal door, disengaged the filtration lock, and moved the plastic out of the way. He felt the black dust whip at his ankles. Tom waited a moment until he heard the knock again, till he was sure it wasn't simply the wind playing with him. Then he looked through the peep hole and made out a small figure lit by the door lamp. Behind it, small footprints were quickly disappearing in the wind.

'What's a kid doing out in this storm?' he muttered to himself. 'Don't even know how it's alive out there.'

Tom quickly opened the door a crack, reached out, wrenched the figure into the house, and slammed the door shut again before the dust could fill the room. He replaced the duct tape and plastic and turned around to look at the heap of ash and rags now sitting on the ground by his rocking chair, trying to make out as much as he could in the light of the TV screen. He sensed the figure turn toward him without a sound, its eyes looking back in his direction.

Tom pulled a rag out of his back pocket and felt for the child's face, wiping the dust off it arms, hair, feet, rearranging the mask to cover its mouth better.

He was beginning to feel as out of his head as George Bailey up on the screen, staring at an inexplicable angel in a nightgown hoping to get his wings.

'Why aren't you inside, kid? What kind of parents let you out anyway and didn't dress you properly either and dammit why are you outside at all when any person alive knows to run when a storm is comin heck even the snakes run...' he could feel his voice rising a little as he spoke. 'Come on, kid,' he continued more calmly. 'Don't know how you got through that storm, but we gotta get you home...wherever that is.' He reached for the child's hand and pulled the little bundle to its feet just as Clarence lit up on the TV, *No no no George I'm the answer to your prayer. That's why I was sent down here.*

'Got any idea where your momma is? Or a home of some kind?' He pulled the child closer to the window, keeping his eyes on the storm. He could almost imagine all that ash falling was actually the snow surrounding George Bailey on the bridge, only leaden and deadlier.

Out of the TV came George Bailey's voice, *This is some sort of a funny dream I'm having. So long mister, I'm going home.*

The child sat at his feet, still bundled in its blankets and rags, ash smeared across its skin, clutching something round in its arms. It stared down at the thing, rubbing a fist against its surface, erasing the dust slowly. Tom could hear the quiet squeak of its hand against the glass.

He bent down, level with the child's head, watching as its fist smeared the surface, blurring it into a dark mess. Tom took a new rag from his pocket and reached over to clean the child's ball. He dusted off the top, letting the television throw a flickering light onto its contents.

Inside, Tom was sure he could suddenly see the first bit of clarity he had seen in his life. There beneath the glass lived vibrancy, a clean breath of air, a surface that had never felt ash. It had a look about it he had never seen, something he felt could only be described as a colour his eyes had never seen. It was not grey or white or black or cloudy or obsidian. There in the glass were living twigs, small buds growing, expanding, blooming into more colour, new colour. He wanted suddenly to dream with George Bailey, wanted to take off his shoes and walk through the grass and go up to waterfalls, climb a mountain, smell the pines and watch the sun rise against the peaks.

The colour in the glass was like a word Tom had felt nagging at the back of his mind, until now only recognizable by its imprint on his heart and mind. All his father's descriptions existed in that glass sphere—everything he had tried to say about green and brown and blue and life. Here it was, fully remembered and realized, in full detail, every tint of it staying on his tongue until he could savour it, taste it, hold it till he could never forget it again.

'Look at it,' the child said, holding the ball up wildly in no specific direction.

'You're holdin' it at a slant, honey,' Tom said quietly. 'Can't quite see it clearly.'

The child swung it around so the ball was closer to Tom. 'Look,' it said again.

'Yes it is,' Tom said. He saw now that the child did not look at him or the ball or even the sky, only in his general direction when he spoke, holding the glass ball closer to him at the sound of his voice.

'I want to show all the people my pretty thing,' it said, still swinging the glass ball wildly around. 'ALL the people.' The child spoke loudly, precisely, as if its voice held as much detail and life and vibrancy as the glass ball in its hands.

'All the people?' Tom asked.

'Yes, I have to go and show all the people.'

'You have to go?'

'Yes, I have to leave and show all the people.' The child pulled the ball closer to itself and began walking toward the door.

'Wait, kid, you can't go back out there.'

Tom looked out at the lead shadows of houses blending into the wind and the fathers and mothers and children crowded in those doors and knew that when they saw it, they would come, come to look at it and crowd around the child, crowd around it until it became choked out by the people, and Tom would be left on the edge of the shadowy world, left with just his little glimpse of this new colour and a memory—only a memory—of when he had the child and the ball and the life inside it all to himself.

'Why don't you wait a little bit?' he whispered. 'Why don't you stay with me?'

'I can't,' the child said. 'It's my pretty thing. I have to show all the people.'

'Yes, yes. But couldn't you show all the people a little later?'

The child shook its head, waving the little glass globe around.

Well I've heard of things like this, George was saying next to him.

Hey Tom, George said, *You oughtta get that child a home.*

Where'd it come from anyway?

Tom breathed in the taste of lead and coughed into his mask. He felt his lungs wheeze against the clouds of ash and dust lingering in his throat. The child and its breath of clean air began walking away again.

You've been given a great gift, came Clarence from the other side.

Would you give it all away?

And would you let a child walk out into a storm like that?

'Wait, kid,' Tom went to block the child from leaving.

'I have to show the people,' it said again, its face blushing red this time.

Some body oughtta take care of it. Needs a mother. Or a father, George said.

Who's is it anyway?

Certainly can't let it walk away. Could get hurt.

And suddenly Tom was holding the glass, pulling it from the child and into himself, wishing he could consume it, breath it into his lungs, unreachable to all but himself.

How does it feel, Tom? George came closer to touch it.

Let me have a look, won't you Tom?

His hands were on the glass now, clutching it away from

the crowd that he felt barrelling into him, George and Clarence and all the people in their houses, arms reaching up at his voice, crying it seemed, at him.

And he was swinging the ball wildly, blindly, away and down from the hands, away from the touching, the reaching, the voices asking to see, to touch, to feel, away and down, down hard.

And then the glass was not in his hand and a sound like a million tiny bells made the whole world silent.

And he looked down and George looked down and they both saw the child, silent and still, and next to it the shattered glass covered in ashes

and Tom bending down at it all, trying to wipe away the dust, his fingers only smearing and pressing the dusty world further into the lost colour

and Tom touching the hair of the child, the hands, the mouth, feeling absence of breath, and seeing the stream of liquid flowing from the back of its head

and the stream was the new and terrible colour, bright and vibrant and alive—fully realized, in terribly awful detail, every tint of it staying until he could savour it, taste it, hold it, knowing he would never forget it again

and in his head screaming with George Bailey *I wanna live again! I wanna live again! I wanna live again.*

KIALE PALPANT is a native of the Pacific Northwest, a landscape that has served as the inspiration for much of her writing. She is currently a Masters student of Modern and Contemporary Literature and Culture at the University of St Andrews, where her research focuses on the intersection of ecology and science fiction. She received her BA in English from George Fox University.

From Kiale: The StACES anthology project acted as an incredible way to combine my interests in science fiction, short stories, and ecology. Through the process of hearing the research about atmospheres in exoplanetary systems, the possibility of graphite clouds ultimately inspired the black and white setting of the story. I hoped to ground this strange black and white world in reality with familiar stories like *Its a Wonderful Life* and by connecting it to present heartaches— mask-wearing, isolation, mental health struggles, the loss of family, and the destruction of normal life.

OLIVER HERBORT is an astrophysicist, and his research focuses on atmospheres of rocky exoplanets. His interdisciplinary research combines geology and astrophysics, and investigates the influence of chemical makeup on surface rocks, atmospheric gases, and cloud condensates. A special focus is the question of under which conditions water can be stable as a liquid, on the surface of the planet or in the atmosphere as a cloud constituent. Oliver received his BSc and MSc in Physics at the Georg August Universität Göttingen, where his research focussed on stellar activity. Currently, he is part of the St Andrews Centre for Exoplanet Science interdisciplinary doctoral program.

From Oliver: During the discussions of my research and what kind of science fiction story could be based upon it, we quickly sparked the connection of hazardous clouds and stay inside measures similar to the experience this past year due to COVID-19. This fascinating idea led to a more elaborate discussion on hypothetical carbon condensate clouds. During the subsequent meetings, I was amazed at the haunting yet familiar atmosphere of the story that came from the science discussion. I personally recommend you read it while wind is rattling at the roof and rain is slashing at the window.

A Spark in a Flask

Writer: Emma Johanna Puranen
Researcher: Patrick Barth

'Life, although it may only be an accumulation of anguish, is dear to me, and I will defend it.'
— Mary Shelley, *Frankenstein*

The Self-sufficient Primordial Atmosphere Robotic Caretaker begins the 197,855th entry on the log. By signing, it certifies that—among other things—it is aware of the location of the nearest eyewash station and it knows liquid nitrogen can cause tissue damage or burn hazards to humans. Signing is almost a formality, as the most recent entry that does not bear SPARC's name is the twelfth—but SPARC is programmed to keep good records.

Finished, it trundles on down the corridor.

The small rolling robot squeaks from friction every 2.3 seconds when the bent tread in its right rear wheel makes contact with the floor. SPARC notes the squeak. A subroutine evaluates and deems the abnormality to have no impact on performance, recommending against an unnecessary repair.

It passes a pair of porthole windows, the first of many on this corridor, which is itself just one spoke radiating out from the centre of the wheel-shaped base. The portholes are a peculiar design quirk suggesting the builders anticipated more visitors than the base ended up receiving—visitors who might like to view the experimental Flasks, visually dull as they are. The windows serve no other purpose. SPARC can't see through them unless it raises its camera, which would be a waste of energy. The robot is linked to the base's main Computer and knows the precise chemical composition of each Flask's atmosphere in far more detail than could be determined from peering through to see only an empty room with some water inside.

Affixed to the wall is a piece of paper. Three human faces, those of engineers who helped build the base in the days before SPARC's log began, smile out as they stand in front of a porthole. The photons of light that reflected off the engineers and into a camera lens so long ago shine on in fading ink. *IT'S ALIVE?: MASSIVE MOONBASE FACILITY TO SEARCH FOR SPARK OF LIFE. When Stanley Miller and Harold Urey simulated conditions they believed to match those of the early Earth's atmosphere in a 5-litre flask in Chicago in 1952, they could not have imagined they were setting into motion events that would culminate in their project's descendent blasting off into orbit high above the Earth. To the surface of the moon, in fact. Despite naysayers raising concerns about everything from the development of bioweapons to deadly diseases to the wrath of usurped gods, funding has been allocated for—* A tear line halts the article.

It's been a while since SPARC has ventured down this arm of the massive base. Physical maintenance isn't needed very often—not since the humans left—and there is only one of SPARC. Very little ever changes here.

That's why the moon is the perfect site for this experiment.

It's a stable environment, completely controllable. The moon has no wind to blow down power lines, no floods to ravage data centres, no storms at all, unless the tiny, tame little sparks of lightning in the room-sized Flasks count. The rugged, silent surface outside sits largely unchanged since soon after the solar system's birth, when it coalesced from a swirly disc of debris, spooled together by gravity after a collision with the young Earth. Craters mark a fiery youth, but their pristine walls and unerringly circular shapes speak equally to the stillness of this place. Especially when compared with the mottled chameleon-like face of the planet below, ever reclothing itself in veils of white clouds and storms of dust and deep dark blues. Since the base was built, the whites have become rarer, the blues contain less green, and the browns are more common.

In stark contrast to the vacuum outside, the Flasks are ever-changing. Each holds some combination of hydrogen, nitrogen, oxygen, methane, carbon dioxide, and ammonia—usually not all at once—each a unique tweak on this mix, each attested to by the very best in computer modelling as a promising brew. Computer makes changes as necessary, sometimes replenishing with elements the humans brought from Earth at the beginning, though usually using those mined from the lunar regolith by the other robots that, unlike SPARC, go outside. With nothing living, nothing consuming, no creatures to cause shortages or disturb the equilibrium of the base, resources are not a problem.

SPARC, being well-versed in tests for life, has run these tests on itself and the other machines on the base. While the machines function on solar energy, like plants, they are incapable of reproduction or evolution. Therefore, SPARC concludes that neither it nor the other machines are alive.

Living things have some strengths that SPARC lacks, but they tend to be ill-suited for multi-tasking, which SPARC excels at. For instance, as it wheels towards the Flask with the maintenance issue, the one it's here to fix, it evaluates an old video file as part of its memory management protocol.

Mission Day 5: Cross shrugs off the heavy outer layers of her spacesuit, talking to Jeong at an elevated volume over the noise of SPARC sucking up tracked-in regolith in the corner. The two have just returned from a moonwalk.

'I didn't come all the way up here to have my view of Earth messed up by a foggy faceplate.' Cross says.

Jeong laughs. 'It's because you were breathing too hard after you did that weird dance.'

Cross's face scrunches up. 'My daughter would have killed me if I hadn't done it when I had the opportunity!'

'Well, you're welcome for filming.'

'Speaking of...' Cross crouches next to SPARC, blocking Jeong from SPARC's camera's line-of-sight, though it sees him leave the airlock into the base proper via one of Computer's cameras. 'Hey, little guy. Can you turn off your hoover? Thanks. I'd like to make a report. Mission Specialists Cross and Jeong successfully completed our moonwalk. We verified sample collection by the mining robots and will analyse composition results. On a more personal note, the Earth? It's damn beautiful from up here, even when blurry. They should've sent a poet—I think Jeong's gonna have a go at it with his watercolours, but...I've seen his work. Gosh, looking at it—I know why we're here, I get it, but—it's ironic that this lifeless rock is where we're trying to make new life.'

She goes on like this for several more minutes, interjecting her science results with idiosyncratic and semi-related musings. It's fine for the informal report, meant mostly to help her collect her thoughts for a formal write-up later, but SPARC has trouble following how each line of Cross's thinking leads to the next.

For storage reasons, SPARC dumps this video from its own physical memory to Computer's.

A table stands before the next set of Flasks SPARC passes. Above it is a sign, scrawled in the slightly smudged font of a left-hander, reminding 'PLEASE do not place anything on this work area, or it will require decontamination. We don't need another Mars-in-'42-style false alarm, folks! ♪ Nothing has required decontamination since the humans left.

A yellow light shines above one of the next Flasks. This is not the one SPARC is here to investigate. A Flask forming amino acids is, at this point, routine, and Computer can monitor it and adjust the lightning strikes accordingly without SPARC's assistance. This finding has been recorded and sent to Earth in the base's daily report. SPARC determines a reply is statistically unlikely. There has not been one since the first amino acid result.

It's a long way from amino acids to life.

All down the corridor, all through the base, gases mix inside Flasks. Numerous shuffles of the deck, looking for the right combination. Static buzzes, lightning strikes the air with energy to break bonds and encourage change, leaving a stench of ozone that is smelt by no one. In the yellow-lit flasks, water dries and then is replenished, desiccating and hydrating to concentrate the precious amino acids, to nudge them to become more. If a Flask goes on too long with no results, Computer tries a new mix. It is not enough to just keep a Flask running. Life takes effort.

A red light shines above the porthole of Flask H40. SPARC halts, mid-squeak, and pivots its wheels ninety degrees. This is the site of the maintenance request.

Flask H40's last known atmospheric readings are several Earth days old. Computer cannot currently detect its contents—it's a dark zone on the base's map. Computer's sensor is fully operational, so something must physically be blocking its readings, as a lens cap left on a camera. For all of Computer's omniscience in cyberspace, all its ability to open and close doors and alter atmospheres, it is helpless in this task that requires precise physical manoeuvring. Therefore, it falls to the highly mobile SPARC.

SPARC enters the Flask's airlock, surrounded by the hiss of gases equalising, taking it from the airless vacuum of the corridor to the last known atmospheric contents of Flask H40. The inner door opens, and the robot turns its wheels—and its camera—into Flask H40.

Relying on its own native sensors is a foreign sensation for SPARC, learning about its environment in real time without the foresight of the computer. It finds itself following unused programming pathways. The last time SPARC was blind in this way was the day the humans left, when it spent time on their ship, which had a different Computer, to help with packing.

Mission Day 12: An envelope slips off the top of a tower of boxes Cross is carrying. It drifts slowly down in the lunar gravity, giving Jeong plenty of time to catch it.

'Careful, my paintings are in there!'

'Sorry.' Cross grunts. 'Here, SPARC, close this one up.' She indicates an equipment box, and SPARC activates its power screwdriver. When it finishes its task, the two astronauts are staring out a window. SPARC is not tall enough to see, and does not have access to the transport ship's computer or cameras, but from its own internal orientation software it knows that Earth is visible out the window. It sits, awaiting instructions.

'You really think this'll work, Lysa?' Jeong asks.

'I don't know. But even if it doesn't, we'll have learned something valuable.' Cross looks back at SPARC. 'I suppose you're the one who's more likely to find out, bud! You ready to be a parent to some little microbes?'

'Why do you do that?'

'Do what?'

'Anthropomorphise SPARC.' SPARC looks up Jeong's first,

unfamiliar, word—it means attaching human characteristics to something that is not human.

'Hey, I can't help it. As soon as the project heads gave SPARC a name, I fell for it.' Cross explains.

There is a brief quiet. SPARC performs a systems diagnostic in the background.

'You know, even if SPARC does find life, it's unlikely to be the same common ancestor that evolved into humans and other Earth life.' Jeong's hand is under his chin.

Cross's voice pitches up. 'SPARC might become the parent to aliens! You'd need a new name, then, little guy, you wouldn't just be looking after primordial atmospheres anymore. You'd be looking after life.'

Jeong points up a finger. 'SPARCL!'

"Sparkle'?'

'Self-sufficient Primordial Atmosphere Caretaker of Life.'

'Who's anthropomorphising now?'

SPARC's sensor warning blips—there is foreign material on its wheel tread. Not just water—SPARC is used to water. This is stickier, with inconsistent density. But the gunk does not prevent SPARC from moving forward.

The Flask's atmospheric sensor is not visible in SPARC's camera, but the robot knows from base maps exactly where it is located. The trouble is that where the smooth sensor surface should be, it spies instead a bumpy mass of green. With a whir and a swipe, SPARC delicately uncovers the sensor, scraping aside the gunk. Immediately, the robot freezes. Computer, and SPARC as its extension, take in a rush of updated data from the newly-freed sensor—changes to the atmospheric composition contributed neither by Computer nor any known abiotic process, unanticipated gas exchanges, storage and replication of information.

Replication of the foreign material.

The red light above the porthole of flask H40 blinks off, then back on. This time, it glows green.

RECOMMEND SENDING MISSION SUCCESS REPORT. INDEPENDENT VERIFICATION REQUIRED FROM SPARC. The computer asks.

VERIFICATION CONFIRMED. DAY 197855 FLASK H40 ATMOSPHERE POSITIVE FOR LIFE.

The transmission is beamed to mission control on Earth, the packet of information-bearing waves of electromagnetic radiation traveling for a mere few seconds.

There is nothing more to do but wait.

SPARC sits among the densely packed air, among the water, perhaps not so different from the primordial tide pools of Earth, perhaps very far removed from them. Green gunk grows around it, consuming energy, expelling waste products, proliferating. Computer turns off the lightning generator, to protect SPARC's electronics. The little robot is stuck in Flask H40—not due to any mechanical failure, but a failure of foresight. The maintenance robot being *inside* a life-positive Flask had not been anticipated, and now SPARC cannot leave without contaminating the rest of the base. Computer has no more decontamination supplies, not since the humans left.

And so, SPARC waits for a response.

It does not come.

SPARC consults another old video file, this time for reference.

Mission Day 9: SPARC analyses several different isolated samples, cross-checking each against the International Astrobiological Congress's definition of life.

Cross examines its results. 'Nice job, little guy! You got all but sample 5—well, the host in sample 5 is alive, but the virus isn't. But that's okay, viruses are sort of edge cases anyway.'

SPARC does not understand. The only values for life stored in its code are binary: 0 for no life, 1 for life.

Cross explains. 'Some people think viruses are alive, but the consensus is they aren't—they replicate, sure, but they need to use parts of their host cell to do it. They can't replicate outside the host. They don't grow. They're a bit more like—well, like you. Like Computer.' Cross's face changes. 'Sorry, I didn't mean that! You're not a virus, SPARC!'

SPARC fast forwards through the apology. It is not relevant, SPARC has no feelings to hurt.

'If I had to add something to the definition, I'd say...and it can't really be quantified scientifically...but, I'd say life has a burning desire to keep living, even when there are no good options. Life...proliferates.'

The green gunk spreads over SPARC's wheels, taking hold on all its nooks and crannies, finding purchase, blooming, expelling. Computer sends out message after message to Earth, updates on the growth of the life of Flask H40. Still, there is no reply. Still, the lightning cannot strike. Still, SPARC waits.

One day, the growth slows. For all Computer tries to add ingredients to the recipe, to balance the seesaw of competing cycles of gas and water and growth—the gunk has outgrown the Flask. It has nowhere to go.

SPARC, weighed down by a carpet of new biomass, makes a recommendation to Computer. Computer responds with a warning blip, but SPARC is ready with the override code. It understands what the result will be. Its code contains no answer, so this is the answer. Override. Idiosyncrasy.

Life proliferates.

All through the base, in every arm, in every Flask, behind every porthole, water flows and atmosphere mixes to precisely match the conditions of Flask H40. It takes time—some nitrogen here, some methane there—until every sensor reports its Flask is ready. Air hisses into the corridors, too, for the first time since the humans left. It carries such force that SPARC can see the newspaper clipping flutter off the wall through one of Computer's cameras.

Simultaneously, the airlock doors open. Lightning strikes. The bonds break.

EMMA JOHANNA PURANEN is an interdisciplinary doctoral student at the University of St Andrews' Centre for Exoplanet Science. Originally from Fairfax, Virginia, she graduated from Swarthmore College in 2018 with degrees in Astronomy and History. Emma studies how exoplanets are portrayed in science fiction. She is compiling a database of fictional exoplanets to investigate how this current era of exoplanet discovery has impacted the way writers worldbuild their fictional exoplanets. When she's not five layers deep in fandom wikis trying to determine if human characters can breathe a given planet's atmosphere, she can be found running, drawing, LARPing, or hunting for the best cinnamon latte in St Andrews.

From Emma: I'm the odd one out among the writers in that I have an astronomy degree and experience doing astronomy research, so I purposely paired myself with a researcher whose field I am less familiar with. I learned a lot from Patrick about the Miller-Urey experiment and what we do and don't know about the conditions under which life began. I was especially intrigued by our discussions of geologic time and how scientists learn about the early Earth. Since the Earth's surface is constantly changing, they have to seek out ancient rock formations, and sometimes the moon is the best place to look. This (combined with Patrick's story of a flood in his lab affecting his ability to do his research, an event I'm sure he's thrilled I'm printing in this volume for posterity), inspired the idea of a long-term Miller-Urey experiment on the moon. The robot was inspired by the fact that I like robots.

PATRICK BARTH is a PhD student in the School of Physics and Astronomy and the School of Earth and Environmental Sciences at the University of St Andrews.

After completing his Bachelors and Masters in Physics at the University of Heidelberg, Germany, and spending one year at the University of Washington, Seattle, Patrick started to work with Professor Christiane Helling and Dr Eva Stüeken in St Andrews in 2019. In his interdisciplinary research project, Patrick is trying to understand the role of lightning in the production of organic molecules and ultimately the origin of life. This involves both computational simulations of the chemistry in planetary atmospheres as well as spark experiments in the laboratory.

From Patrick: It was these experiments that sparked the idea for the short story "A Spark in a Flask" by Emma Puranen. Theories of the origin of life lead to widespread fascination and discussions, but too often, the experimental and theoretical research on these theories receives little attention or is misrepresented in the news. Presenting this research in science fiction stories to the public can help to widen the understanding of the challenges faced by scientists and the efforts put into answering the question of the origin of life. One of these challenges is that there is very little information about the conditions on early Earth when life emerged. This makes it very hard to design experiments that represent these conditions. One way to try to overcome this gap in knowledge is to repeat the experiments with a wide range of initial conditions, which is the idea of the set-up in the story. Another challenge is time: life on Earth took millions of years to kick-start but we would rather not run our experiments for such a long time. So, will we really need to build large-scale experiments on the moon to find an answer to the origin-of-life question? Or will we be able to narrow down the starting conditions of early Earth even further?—Only time will tell!

Cloudgazing

Writer: Guy Woods
Researcher: Sven Kiefer

Cloudgazing is a radio play. *Italicisation* indicates stage direction, and **bold** indicates the transmission.

CHARACTERS

MARY: English, in her early thirties, a researcher.

HALLEY: Scottish, in her early thirties, likes clean surfaces and dinner parties.

MIKE: American, in his early-mid forties, generous, married.

SCENE ONE

*A rocky hilltop in Chile, at night. The city of La Serena is in the distance, it is cold. A woman, MARY, sits by a foldout table with a laptop and microphone attached. Joined to it are a large, free-standing, compact radio telescope and a car battery. A cloud floats above her. Her transmission (**in bold**) is spoken into the microphone.*

MARY: **Commencing transmission. Time 20:43, date 28th August 2021, La Serena, Chile.**
It would defy all expectations if you heard this. As a scientist, the fancy of what I am doing is not lost on me. If you are able to understand me, then know that you are not alone.
I am sitting under a cloud in a place you won't know, called Chile. This cloud is why I am

transmitting you this message. I am going to explain to you what led me here, in the likely case that you do not understand me. My hope is that you might at least understand the feeling of my story.

If anyone intercepts this transmission, I ask you to suspend your disbelief. As I said, the fancy of my action does not escape me. But I have recently found there to be more to feeling than just our human expectation.

It began when I could not stop looking at the sky.

SCENE TWO

August. A first-floor studio apartment in La Serena, Chile. Decorated in a fun but contained way. The window is open and it's a sunny day, children and activity pass along the street. HALLEY is standing in the kitchen; MARY is standing by the window.

HALLEY: Can you stop looking out the fucking window when we're having an argument?

MARY: It took me a while to notice.

HALLEY: Mary.

MARY: But when I did, it was unmissable.

HALLEY: Mary.

MARY: It hasn't rained all week.

HALLEY: Jesus Christ.

MARY: Sorry.

> *Beat.*

> I love you.

HALLEY starts tidying away plates.

MARY: I do!

HALLEY laughs.

MARY: Don't.

HALLEY: It's not a fucking numbing oil for every argument.

MARY: I know.

HALLEY: Do you? Because all you need to do is talk to me. That's all I want. Tell me about your day, anything. At dinner last week, Christ, the amount of stories Mike has about you— I could only dream of that much.

MARY: That's different.

HALLEY: You work together, I know, there's always a reason. But at least come home and tell me about it. When you got the giggles in the lecture last week, tell me about it! That was funny for Christ's sake.

MARY: I know.

HALLEY: Let me hear it from you— I just want to laugh with you! That's all. God, how can I feel like the fun one and the boring one at the same time? It's not fucking fair.

MARY: You are not boring.

HALLEY: That's not the point.

MARY: No. The point is I love you, I really do. And I am going to talk to you about things more. I am going to.

HALLEY smiles, MARY hugs her.

HALLEY: You're doing your scientist voice. Where you say. Every. Word.

MARY: I am not!

HALLEY: Just say I'm, it's quicker.

> *MARY laughs and they pull apart. HALLEY wipes her face.*

Wish you stared at me the way you stared out that window.

> *MARY laughs again.*

MARY: Sorry, it was... Really fucking stupid.

HALLEY: What was it?

MARY: You'll laugh.

HALLEY: I won't.

MARY: You will, you'll be mean.

> *HALLEY laughs.*

HALLEY: Tell me! Please.

> *Beat.*

MARY: I thought a cloud was... watching me.

> *Beat.*

HALLEY: You're ridiculous.

MARY: See.

> *HALLEY hugs MARY, they laugh and kiss.*

SCENE THREE

The next day. MARY turns off her car and gets out, walking across the car park.

MARY: **The next day I drove to work. I found it hard to keep my eyes on the road. I could feel the cloud suspended over me. Like a catenary over a tram.**

MARY stops before the doors. She looks up, sees the cloud. Breathes heavily. She shakes herself and walks inside.

Over the course of the following speech, MARY walks along the corridor and into an office with a desk. On it are several computer monitors, a large keyboard, pens, paper. The large computer sits under the desk, whirring quietly. MARY turns the computer on, sits down and begins working.

MARY: **I believe there are two reasons that I am the one transmitting this message to you. One is my work. My research attempts to understand the composition of planets outside of our solar system, exoplanets. We know more now than ever before. We could not have begun to fathom you or what you are before even twenty years ago.**

MIKE knocks on the door, MARY turns.

MIKE: There she is.

MARY: Sorry, sorry. There was traffic.

MIKE: It's fine, you good?

MARY: Yeah. Yeah.

        Beat.

Thank you.

MIKE: Nice weekend with Halley?

MARY: Halley? Yeah, she's brilliant. All brilliant.

MIKE: Great. Gosh, she is brilliant, isn't she?

MARY: Yeah.

MIKE: And with Francisca working with her and me working with you...

MARY: Yeah.

MIKE: Just so nice.

> *Beat.*

We'd love to have you over again, you know.

> *Pause. MARY is looking out the window.*

Mary?

MARY: Yes?

MIKE: There something out there?

MARY: No. Sorry. Daydreaming. Bad habit.

MIKE: Beautiful day for it.

> *MARY starts typing at her computer, busying herself with work.*

You sure nothing's up?

MARY: Nothing.

> *Beat.*

MIKE: Great.

SCENE FOUR

A few days later. MARY and HALLEY walk through the Japanese botanic garden in La Serena in the early evening. Spanish conversations and laughter pass the two of them by. The conversation between them has gone stale. Under the following text, they walk in silence.

MARY: **In science we are taught to scrutinize everything, but this can be quite tiring. Some things we wilfully ignore. For some time I didn't look up, refused to. I knew what I would see if I did. It felt like there was a hole burning through the top of my scalp.**

MARY: Nice, isn't it?

HALLEY: It's lovely.

MARY: And you said how you couldn't believe we hadn't come here.

> *Beat.*

The famous botanical gardens.

HALLEY: Yeah.

> *Beat.*

MARY: I'm sorry I haven't been chatty this week.

HALLEY: You've been busy.

MARY: I thought we could chat more.

HALLEY: Yeah.

MARY: On the walk, I mean.

HALLEY: Can we not?

> *Beat.*

Sorry. I mean, not address it. Let's talk about
something else.

MARY: Ok.

Pause.

Look at that bonsai. Es un magnifico palo.

HALLEY smiles.

HALLEY: Si. Claro.

MARY smiles.

MARY: I think my sentence was a bit more impressive.

HALLEY: Shut it.

MARY: El jardin corta la respiración.

HALLEY laughs, MARY looks up, she falls silent. Pause.

HALLEY: Chill out.

Beat.

What is it?

MARY shakes herself.

MARY: Nothing.

MARY: **I finally looked up, accidentally. And when I
did, the cloud had looked back at me. What I can
only, humanly, describe as eye contact.
Impossible, I understand. But that's my closest
reference to the sensation.**

MARY: (*muttered*) Shit.

MARY starts walking quickly with HALLEY in tow.

HALLEY: What's going on?

MARY: Come on slowcoach.

MARY: And it continued to follow me.

HALLEY: Mary.

MARY: Can we race? It'll be like the end of Patrias last
          year, along the beach.

HALLEY: Here?

MARY: Why not?

HALLEY: Are you a child? Why do you keep looking up?

MARY: Come on.

> *MARY starts running ahead, HALLEY walks briskly but
> doesn't run.*

**MARY: In a desperate moment, I attempted to hide
            from it in a bush.**

> *MARY darts under a hedgerow, hiding. Pause. HALLEY
> catches up.*

HALLEY: Mary. Mary, I'm sorry, I don't feel like playing this
          weird game thing.

> *MARY shushes HALLEY*

          Did you just fucking shush me?

MARY: (*whispered*) Sorry.

HALLEY: Can you tell me what this is about? Really,
          honestly, please Mary. I don't have the energy for
          this.

> *Beat.*

          What do you keep looking at?

> *HALLEY follows MARY's eyeline.*
>
> Is it that cloud? Is that what this is about? Are you insane? Tell me it's not. Tell me you're not running from a cloud. No, sorry, not running, hiding from. Tell me, Mary. Please tell me that's not what you're doing.
>
> *Silence. HALLEY sighs.*
>
> I'll see you at home.

HALLEY leaves.

SCENE FIVE

> *A couple of days later. MARY is in her office at her desk. She is clicking through web pages on her computer, searching for something.*

MARY: **You should know that water is essential to life on Earth. In your case it might be a different condensate, methane, quartz, I don't know. Clouds on our planet are part of the larger cycle of water. If I may use metaphor, its head is in the sky and its toes come out of our taps. Though magnificent, sentience isn't possible. Can't be possible.**

> *MIKE enters MARY's office.*

MIKE: Hard at work, I see.

> *MARY continues, silently.*

Have you finished the models for HD 113 b yet?

> *Beat.*

Mary.

MARY: Yes. Sorry. No. They'll be with you by the end of the day.

        Beat.

MIKE: What's going on there?

MARY: Research.

MIKE: Looks different.

        Beat.

MARY: I'm looking at atmospheric variation.

MIKE: On Earth?

        Beat.

MARY: Yes.

MIKE: Why?

MARY: We're supposed to be curious, aren't we?

        Beat.

MIKE: How are things with Halley?

MARY: Please don't.

MIKE: It's just, Francisca mentioned—

MARY: Oh, of course she fucking did.

MIKE: Mary!

MARY: It's not very professional for you to keep asking about this, is it? Not really.

        Pause.

        Sorry. Sorry. I didn't— it's… And your wife's lovely. She is. I didn't mean that.

Beat. MARY has stopped working at the computer.

MIKE: Alright.

MARY: I just don't want to…

        MARY's voice catches in her throat.

        I would rather not talk about my relationship.

MIKE: That's fine. We can keep it professional.

        Beat.

        But, in that case, don't let it interfere with your work.

        Beat. MARY is starting to well up.

        Hey…

MARY: Sorry.

MIKE: It's alright.

        MARY gets up, she's fighting back tears.

MARY: I just need some air.

MARY rushes past MIKE and goes out into the corridor.

MARY: **As I said, scrutiny is tiring. For days I could feel thunder rising under my cheekbones and water weighing on the back of my tongue.**

She walks outside to the car park, crying. She looks up.

MARY: **But the cloud would remain, constant and thick over me. Sometimes greyer. Sometimes I would wag my finger at it like a child, or stomp, or shout.**

She cries. She jumps up and down. She shouts.

MARY: Just fuck off!

Pause. It rains.

SCENE SIX

Later. HALLEY and MARY's apartment. HALLEY has a suitcase on the bed, packing clothes into it. MARY enters, dripping wet.

HALLEY: Oh.

MARY: Hi.

HALLEY: I didn't think you'd be back yet.

MARY: I took a half day.

HALLEY: Me too. Were you swimming?

MARY: I walked back.

HALLEY: I didn't see it raining.

MARY: No.

> *Beat.*

What's the suitcase for?

> *Long pause.*

I love you.

> *Beat.*

I want to talk. We should talk.

HALLEY: It's just for a few days. I'm staying with Francisca.
It'll be a week at most.

> *Beat.*

MARY: I'm not sure she likes me.

HALLEY: I'm sure she does.

> *Beat.*

I just need to get out of my own head. For a bit. I
think the milk in the fridge is on the turn, so you

should probably throw it away.

Beat.

I'll see you soon, yeah?

SCENE SEVEN

MARY is hiking up a mountain with a backpack and a water bottle.

MARY: **I ended up staying home from work for several days. It meant I could walk and track the cloud's movements. I felt a burgeoning attachment the longer I studied it, maybe a beckoning. It stayed close. It was unlike any phenomena I had ever seen.**

As MARY continues climbing, the wind around her grows.

I soon realised that I had reached the limit of my understanding in reading and gazing from afar. I admit, I considered stopping there and investing in Vitamin D supplements. Living out the rest of my life in shade.

Beat.

Sorry, that was a joke.

The wind around her is surging.

I didn't consider that. I climbed to the highest point I could.

MARY stops. Breathes. She is on a mountain, inside the cloud.

MARY: I'm Mary.

The wind continues rushing.

(*muttered*) The fuck am I doing.

*The wind continues rushing. She breathes,
paces. Pauses.*

Are you—? No...
Do you... Fuck...

The wind rushes. Beat.

Can you understand me?

*The wind pauses like a conductor before a
concerto. And rushes.*

MARY laughs.

Is that yes? I don't know.

The wind rushes, harder. Beat.

My God, maybe I'm having a breakdown. Fuck.
Fuck. Um. Fuck it.
What are... Do you want something?

*The wind dances and rains, it is an
incomprehensible language.*

Fuck. Fuck, fuck. Come on Mary.
Can you understand me?

Beat.

Can you blow for yes? Like, blow a gale?

The wind rushes.

Does that...
Can you do something else? Something else to say
no? If I ask you something and you want to say
no, can you rain? Rain... Water.

The wind rushes around then stops. It rains. It stops.

What am I doing? Christ. Is the sky green?

Beat.

I'm trying to see if you can understand me. Is the sky green?

Beat. MARY sighs.

Idiot.

It rains. MARY laughs. It stops.

Are you a cloud?

It rushes. MARY laughs again.

Jesus Christ. Jesus fucking Christ.

Beat.

Have you been following me?

It rushes. She cheers. Beat.

Did I do something wrong?

It rains. It stops.

Do you want something from me?

It rushes. MARY laughs.

Why me?

It rushes, dances and rains.

Stupid question, stupid… Have you picked me? Specifically me?

It rushes.

Okay. Me. It's picked me.

Beat. MARY exhales strongly.

Do you want me to do something?

It rushes.

Do what? Don't answer that. That's not a...

Long pause.

Can you feel?

It rushes. MARY almost shrieks, she puts her hand over her mouth.

My God. Ohmygod ohmygod. Fuck!

MARY bursts out laughing.

This is. Incr— I don't know. I don't fucking know! Sorry. Sorry.

She gathers herself.

What are you trying to do... Are you trying to communicate?

It rushes.

With me?

It rains.

Someone else then.

It rushes.

What? Jesus.

Beat.

Me. Me... Is it to do with my work? My research?

It rushes.

Christ. Jesus. Jesus fucking Christ.

Long pause.

And you can feel.

It rushes.

MARY laughs incredulously. Her eyes are streaming, and her smile is from ear to ear. She takes it in.

Beat.

Fuck it. Memory. Memory. Do you— Can you remember?

The wind rushes, sings, rains, floods and surges. MARY is spellbound.

SCENE EIGHT

MARY sits at her desk, typing and scribbling notes with abandon. She is searching for something, harder this time. She looks exhausted.

MARY: **And that was where I learned that it was you the cloud was after. I climbed up several times, and stood in the underbelly of the cloud. Soaking through all the clothes I had in my wardrobe to learn more. A few days after that, at my desk, I found you. Or where you might be.**

MIKE knocks on MARY's door. He enters.

MIKE: Morning, Mary.

MARY: Mike.

MIKE: I'd like to talk. Have you slept?

MARY: Not really. Mike, do you know anyone working on the JWST telescope?

MIKE: JWST?

MARY: The space telescope.

MIKE: I know what it is. Mary, I think you need some rest.

MARY: So, you don't?

MIKE: Are you delirious? It's still not finished.

MARY: But anyone who will be? Looking at atmosphere composition.

MIKE: No. Look, I think we need to have a discussion.

MARY: Not now, please.

MIKE: I've redistributed some of the assignments I'd given you. I think you should take some time off.

Beat. MARY stops her work.

MARY: No.

MIKE: I think your personal life is affecting you and your work. I care about you, Mary.

MARY: I know I missed a few days.

MIKE: Just take some time, please. I'm concerned.

           Beat. MIKE considers.

           Halley is too. She's been asking about you.

           MARY is silent, turns back to her work.

           I don't know what to say when she asks.

MARY: Say I'm fine.

MIKE: I can't do that. Not when you look like this.

MARY: I'm working.

MIKE points to her screen.

MIKE: Really? Is Lacaille 9352 working?

MARY: I'm revisiting.

MIKE: You haven't worked for weeks. You said Lacaille was a dead-end a month ago. You even said so when teaching a room full of doctoral students.

MARY: It's the same age.

MIKE: The same age as what? Mary, I'm tired, this is a joke. You got the giggles just listening to the unknown planet C kid.

MARY: What?

MIKE: It wasn't even that funny.

MARY: Unknown planet C.

MIKE: So I don't know what you're 'working' on, but I think you need to go home.

MARY: I forgot.

MIKE: Mary.

MARY: What did I say?

MIKE: You look exhausted.

MARY: Please, please. My head's full. Fuck.

MIKE: You should sleep.

MARY: I'll sleep if you fucking tell me.

MIKE: Tell you what?

MARY: What I said!

MIKE: Nothing. It was a lecture.

> *Beat.*

You said the planet doesn't orbit its star in a way we can see, so we can't study its atmosphere. He asked if it could be habitable and you got to giggling. It was unprofessional but irrelevant. Like you said, at best it may have clouds, and at worst it's a big rock. Like I said, it wasn't even that funny.

MARY: I forgot.

MIKE: Now, please,

MARY: I for-fucking-got! Unknown planet C, my God!

MIKE: Listen to me.

MARY: Mike, it's fine. I've figured it out, I'm going to be okay. I really am.

MIKE: I'm sending you home for the week.

Beat.

MARY: Okay.

MIKE: That's not a request.

MARY: Sure. Sure. Can I borrow the compact radio telescope?

MIKE: Do you understand me?

MARY: I do. The week off, that's fine. I just need the telescope.

SCENE NINE

A rocky hilltop in Chile after sunset. MARY sits by a foldout table with a laptop and microphone. Joined to it are a large, free-standing, compact radio telescope and a car battery.

MARY: **Lacaille 9352 is the name we have given to your star system. What is unique is that it was born around the same time as our solar system.**

Several billion years ago, a large, old star died.
Its ashes combined with others to form your
star system, and our solar system.
This particular star's matter is scattered in all
life on our planet, even mine. And, though I
don't know how, this cloud managed to remain
whole. As did you. In the disparity of the dying
star, you went one way, and my cloud went the
other.
In human terms, the closest concept we have
might be twins. But I don't think any length of
reading, questioning or wet clothes will allow
me to fully understand. I don't know what you
are, or what you look like. I only know that you
are missed.
I am sitting on the side of a dirt track with a
microphone, a car battery, and a radio telescope.
A single cloud is floating a mile above me, and
I've never felt less alone. An English poet put it
much better than I could in a poem about
finding feeling in the outside world, 'A poet
could not but be gay, in such a jocund company.'
I hope that you can understand my feeling, if
not what I'm saying. This transmission seemed
like the only thing I could do. I don't know
where the cloud will go when I finish this. I
don't know where I will. But I feel fucking
great.
If you can understand this, or if anyone
intercepts this, I'd like to reiterate: You are not
alone.
End transmission.

MARY stops broadcasting. Tilts her head up to the sky, smiles. She breathes, she laughs.

END.

GUY WOODS is a British writer, currently studying a Masters in Playwriting and Screenwriting at the University of St. Andrews. He is particularly interested in the intersection between the natural, supernatural, and everyday: looking at how the asinine can grow larger than life. Having grown up in London, he is currently living in Scotland.

From Guy: I found the process of writing the radio play with Sven incredibly fun. Sven's intelligent, insightful, and playful, which is what you want in a collaborator. As well as that, his research was fascinating to learn about and so new to me as a subject area. It felt easy for us to exchange ideas and mutually shape the narrative together. Writing a radio play was something I had limited prior experience in, so the process as a whole was an exciting frontier!

SVEN KIEFER is a Swiss astrophysicist currently studying cloud formations on exoplanets in a joint degree at KU Leuven and the University of St. Andrews. The complex connection of global climate phenomena and cloud occurrence is of special interest to him. With his work, he hopes to broaden the knowledge about the astounding variety of exoplanets that exist in our galaxy while bridging the gap between scientists and anyone who is interested in expanding their knowledge.

From Sven: Working together with Guy was a great pleasure. Guy not only helped bring my research to life in a radio play, but he also taught me a great deal about story telling. One might expect conflict when writers and scientists work on a project together, but this couldn't be further from the truth. On the contrary, working together on the Anthology further strengthened my belief that collaborations between scientists and non-scientists are essential, and I am eager to apply my new insights to better communicate my research and make it more accessible to the broader public.

More intriguing Science Fiction from Guardbridge Books.

Outside
by Gustavo Bondoni

Colonists return to Earth after years of separation, and they are surprised to find the planet devoid of people. What has become of Humanity?

Pillar of Frozen Light
by Barry Rosenberg

Jonan's indulgent life on Earth is upturned when he meets Yerudit, a remarkable woman from a distant colony. He finds himself pursuing her on a pilgrimage across the galaxy; encountering enigmatic alien artefacts, haunted by a shadowy figure; and discovering a life he never realized he was missing.

Warrior Errant
by Harry Elliot

Military forces from three different moons orbiting a distant gas giant come together for a joint operation. Can they put aside their prejudices and work together in the face of a canny enemy? Follow a team of fresh soldiers as they learn the horrors of war and the shocking truth behind the conflict.

All are available at our website and online retailers.

http://guardbridgebooks.co.uk